MISSION OF HOPE

(Branyrd the Angel
Series Book 4)

J.E. SPINA

PUBLISHED BY J.E. SPINA

COPYRIGHT 2024
J.E. Spina
Londonderry, New Hampshire

COVER BY JOHN SPINA

ALL RIGHTS RESERVED

ISBN (paperback)979-8-9874646-3-2

Library of Congress Control Number: 2024920786

Thank you for respecting the hard work of this author.

This book is a work of fiction. Any references to persons, places or things are purely coincidental. Names, characters, places, and events are products of this author's imagination.

ACKNOWLEDGEMENTS

A very special thank you to my incomparable beta readers, Patricia Bradley, Michele Rolfe, and John Spina for working tirelessly to read and review my work and for their helpful input. Their assistance is invaluable and appreciated.

Thank you to my husband, John, for the beautiful cover and for all the dinners he cooked that made it possible for me to continue to write.

DEDICATION

To my best friend, Fran, who is always there to support me, thank you, and may God bless you!

To all who believe in Angels around us

Table of Contents

PUBLISHED BY J.E. SPINA 2

   COPYRIGHT 2024 2

ACKNOWLEDGEMENTS 4

DEDICATION 5

PREFACE 8

CHAPTER ONE 10

CHAPTER TWO 12

CHAPTER THREE 15

CHAPTER FOUR 19

CHAPTER FIVE 24

CHAPTER SIX 29

CHAPTER SEVEN 33

CHAPTER EIGHT 38

CHAPTER NINE 43

CHAPTER TEN 48

CHAPTER ELEVEN 53

CHAPTER TWELVE 57

CHAPTER THIRTEEN 63

CHAPTER FOURTEEN 68

CHAPTER FIFTEEN 73

CHAPTER SIXTEEN 79

CHAPTER SEVENTEEN 83

CHAPTER EIGHTEEN 89

CHAPTER NINETEEN 94

CHAPTER TWENTY 101

CHAPTER TWENTY-ONE 108

CHAPTER TWENTY-TWO 112

CHAPTER TWENTY-THREE 120

CHAPTER TWENTY-FOUR 126

CHAPTER TWENTY-FIVE 132

CHAPTER TWENTY-SIX 138

CHAPTER TWENTY-SEVEN...145

CHAPTER TWENTY-EIGHT 153

CHAPTER TWENTY-NINE 158

CHAPTER THIRTY 165

CHAPTER THIRTY-ONE 170

CHAPTER THIRTY-TWO 178

CHAPTER THIRTY-THREE 183

CHAPTER THIRTY-FOUR 190

CHAPTER THIRTY-FIVE 196

CHAPTER THIRTY-SIX 199

EPILOGUE 204

ABOUT THE AUTHOR 208

A NOTE FROM THE AUTHOR 210

OTHER MG/PT/YA BOOKS BY JANICE SPINA for 10+
....212

YA BOOKS BY JANICE SPINA for 15+ 215

BOOKS BY J.E. SPINA FOR 18+ 216

PREFACE

There are things in this book that cannot be explained to younger children, making this suitable for ages 15+. We all make mistakes but it is how we turn our lives around to correct them that matters. That is what Branyrd must do, not only for herself, but also for others.

This is the fourth book in the series. Even though each book is a stand-alone story dealing in a new mission for the main protagonist; it is important to begin with book 1 to get into the character, Branyrd, and how she matures.

This genre is different from what I have written in the past. I wanted to combine good and evil in a new way through the eyes of an Angel named Branyrd. If you noticed, I capitalize the word Angel everywhere to make it stand out.

Some may believe in Angels on Earth while others are naysayers. I, for one, believe there is something greater than we are out there that is helping us along our troubled paths and trying to steer us in the right direction. We all need help at one time or another in our lives. Some of you may, at one time or another, have had your lives touched by an Angel as I have.

Believe what you may but after reading about this Angel you just may change your mind about believing. I pray this story about Branyrd lightens your hearts, lifts your spirits, gives you hope, and brings a little joy your way.

I wrote this story for all who are trying to find a new home, escape persecution, bigotry, or injustice, to let them know that HE is watching over them and sending help in the form of an Angel.

CHAPTER ONE

Many people were pushing their way through some barriers at the borders of many of the states of this wide country to find new homes. They were too numerous to count.

Men, women, and children were exhausted from the many miles they had to traverse in order to escape their lands from danger and oppression. All they wanted was to be free from tyranny and bring up their children in an environment that was safe.

People came from all over the world when they heard that there was a place that could offer them everything they needed. There were also those who were not to be trusted, murderers, drug lords, human traffickers, and convicted felons who mixed in with the innocent ones.

What the innocent ones didn't expect was these dangerous individuals, who preyed on them during their travels, would try to prevent them from finding a new home. Many of the families would not make it due to illness, death by the hands of these people when they couldn't pay their way, or if they gave up and returned home to face tyranny once again.

Suddenly a little child stumbled and was caught by his mother before he could fall into the river and drown. The father was ahead of them leading their two older children across the water to the other side which was freedom.

In the next second the father tripped, knocked his head on a rock and disappeared under the swiftly moving water while his two children tried in vain to save him. The wife and young child hurried forward to get to him, too, but failed. The older children managed to cross over with their mother and toddler. They stood there looking back at the water, but there was no sign of their father.

***

The LORD looked on with tears in HIS eyes as HE reached forward to comfort the family. HE waved HIS hands over them and they sighed as if they had felt HIS touch. The father now stood at the LORD'S side and watched his family cross into this new land of freedom without him.

HE called out to Benedicto, Guardian Angel on High, to bring Branyrd to HIM. There was much to be done.

CHAPTER TWO

Benedicto searched for Branyrd at her usual cloud base but she wasn't there. He went from cloud to cloud until he finally found her. He could have easily called out to her and she would have had to come to him but he wanted to see what she was up to for himself. He knew how secretive she could be.

"There you are, Branyrd. I've been looking for you."

"You have? I didn't hear you calling me, Benedicto."

"I could have called you but I wanted to see what you were doing and where your latest hideaway was."

"I don't have a hideaway, Guardian Angel. I like to drift back and forth and visit with friends. I knew that I would be leaving sooner or later and wanted to catch up with them."

"Hmm, I see. Did you catch up thoroughly?"

"Yes, I did. Thank you. Does the LORD have a new mission for me?"

"Why yes, HE does. That is why I am here."

"Hmm, I figured as much," Branyrd giggled as she looked at her favorite Guardian Angel with her biggest, brightest smile that lit up Heaven around them. Her wings glistened, spread out around her, and her golden halo lit up the sky as her long golden tresses fell beyond her shoulders.

"You are my favorite Angel, but don't tell the others."

"No worries, Benedicto. They already know that," Branyrd laughed out loud especially after she saw the Guardian Angel's quizzical expression.

"Really? Do they already know that? How can you be sure?"

"Oh, Benedicto, you are such a teaser. Well, what is the new mission about and where are we going?"

"Not so fast, Angel. You need to see HIM for the instructions as usual and HE will tell you everything you need to know."

"Aren't you coming with me?"

"I will be along shortly. I have a few things to take care of, Branyrd. Don't be so worried. You will be able to handle anything that HE gives you. Remember, you are not a newbie Angel anymore. You have already handled three difficult missions."

"Ahh, I know, but I am still nervous just the same, Benedicto. Besides, I couldn't have done any of it without your assistance."

"Don't be too sure of that, Angel. You are mighty and powerful on your own. You have learned so many things and now you can fly on Earth."

"Yes, I can fly! That is the greatest accomplishment so far for me. I didn't think I would ever be able to do that. But I still need you as my sidekick and support. You give me courage when things get tough."

"Do I do all that? I didn't realize that you needed me. You appear to be self-sufficient."

"Well, not entirely, Guardian Angel. I need you. I do love having you along. Please promise that you will come with me again," Branyrd pleaded with eyes sparkling and growing wider.

"Go along now. I will see you soon but only if HE commands that I go along with you."

"But, why wouldn't HE? Benedicto…."

Branyrd sighed and spread her ever-growing wings and flew to the LORD'S Hall.

CHAPTER THREE

The LORD looked down on Branyrd from HIS high seat in HIS kingdom. HE smiled at her and told her to rise up so HE could see her eyes.

Ahh, there you are, Angel. It is good to see you again. You have had three successful missions so far. Are you ready for the next one?"

"Oh, yes, my LORD. I am ready!" Branyrd's voice shook but she felt sure that she was ready if Benedicto could escort her once again. Her thoughts were whirling around in her head.

"Yes, Benedicto will be accompanying you again, Angel. No worries, even though you are more than capable of doing this mission all by yourself. Remember, I am always here for you. All you have to do is call MY name." Branyrd shook after hearing this. She had forgotten that HE could read her thoughts.

"Yes, LORD, I do remember that but I appreciate having my Guardian Angel along to bolster up my confidence that does wane at times."

"Hmm, I see. Well, would you like to have a bird's eye view of what to expect on Earth?"

"Yes, please, LORD. I am anxious to see what I will be doing."

HE opened a window for her to look through. Branyrd patiently waited for the window to clear.

What she saw was shocking. There were many people rushing forward through barriers and crossing a wide river. Some of these people stumbled and drowned, including young children. She saw a man go under the water and not come back up while his family searched in vain for him. This family and many others did manage to make it to safety. They kept moving until they found a place to hide.

She gasped and shook her head. "This can't be happening!"

"Yes, but it is, Angel."

"Why are these people going to this place? Why are they crossing this water? It is too dangerous."

"Yes, but where they are coming from is even more dangerous."

The LORD explained, "Their own homes are no longer safe for them to live in because of war and criminals, who preyed upon them."

"That is a terrible thing. Everyone should have a safe place to live and bring up their children. Isn't that right, LORD?"

"Yes, it should be that way. But there are many who will take what is not theirs so that they will have more for themselves, thereafter making life impossible for others."

"Where are the police to help these people?"

"There aren't enough of them to handle this on their own. That will be your job to try to help them and the people find their way. There will be many obstacles that you will have to face to make life better for everyone you come into contact with."

"But how can I do this for so many, LORD?"

"You will find a way, Angel, but that is not all you will be dealing with. Look at this." HE pointed to the window once again.

There were stores being destroyed by people who broke the windows and tore down the doors to get inside. They were seen coming out of these stores with arms full of all kinds of products, clothes, food, etc.

Branyrd watched in horror as these people raced away to waiting cars as the police were powerless to chase and arrest them all or curtail the damages and return the stolen products to the store owners.

Before Branyrd could respond another window was opened and she saw people shooting other people who were running away from another scene of demonstrations and rioting.

"Why are they shooting all those people? What did they do to deserve that?"

The window was still open and showed a courtroom with a man who was on trial for murdering a child. He was put in jail but then let go shortly thereafter without any punishment.

"What is happening here on Earth, LORD? This is not a good place to live anymore. Why are there so many evil people doing these terrible things without having to pay for their crimes?"

"That is what is making ME so sad. I feel the pain of those who are suffering and know that I must intercede to make it right but I cannot do that. They need to work this out themselves. That is why I am sending you down there to help them make the right decisions and clean up the evil that is growing stronger every day."

"I can feel it too, LORD, the evil I mean. It is quite strong and makes me feel sick. How can I overpower all this evil and make it right for the innocent?"

The LORD waved his hands over Branyrd and floated away from view. In front of her now stood Benedicto who pointed the way for her to go.

"Are you ready to face your next mission, Branyrd?"

"Do I have a choice? This is going to be a multifaceted mission, Benedicto. I don't know if I am strong enough to face the evil that is there."

"You will find the strength, Angel. This is going to be a Mission of Hope for all."

CHAPTER FOUR

Benedicto took Branyrd by the hand and after the LORD outfitted them appropriately in the attire that would blend them into the environment that they would be facing, they descended through the clouds and onto Earth.

Branyrd found herself in a field that bordered the river that she had seen in the LORD'S window. She watched as a woman with three children came toward her. This was the woman who was in the river with her child. The same woman whose husband had drowned.

The woman came up to her and pleaded, "Can you help me please?"

Branyrd looked at the woman with tears in her own eyes matching those of the woman's and took her hand. She spoke softly, "Come with me. I will find you a place of safety for you and your children."

The woman cried openly now as her three children held onto her. "My husband…"

"Yes, I know. HE told me. HE sent me here to help you and others find your way. Please come with me now. We must hurry. There are many others coming this way now."

Branyrd took the woman's hand and the children followed close behind, holding onto their mother and each other. The woman's tears were flowing as she followed the beautiful woman. She thought of what this woman just said to her, something about HE knew. Does she mean GOD? Has GOD not forgotten us?

***

As they walked, Branyrd prayed for guidance as to where she could find a safe respite for the woman and her family until she could find something more permanent.

HE answered her prayer by pointing the way with the breeze that revealed a house behind some trees a short distance away. She hurried the family toward the house and silently thanked HIM.

"Is this a safe place for us to stay?" the woman asked with frightened eyes.

"Yes, for now it is. Come quickly before others follow us."

Branyrd looked behind her for anyone who was coming close. She could hear voices in the distance and the sound of feet pounding the ground which shook from the weight.

They reached the place which was a small shingled, run-down house, its paint was peeling and the shutters were askew. It appeared to be deserted but the Angel crept closer to make sure.

Branyrd stepped up to the door and knocked as she whispered to the family to be quiet. No one came after the third knock. She tried the door and it opened with a squeak, in dire need of some oil.

As the door swung inward the interior was small as was the outside and too dark to see much. They stepped in and squinted their eyes to get accustomed to the lack of light.

They moved silently through the foyer and into the nearest room which was a living area with shadows revealing a couch and two chairs along the wall with a coffee table and two end tables with lamps.

Branyrd moved into the room and went right to the lamps and turned them on. Much to their surprise the lights worked and cast a dim light to the room. The children rushed forward and lay down on the couch to rest. The mother tried to stop them but Branyrd held up her hand and smiled. "It's okay for them to rest. You and I can check the rest of the house together."

The woman nodded and followed Branyrd from room to room. There were only three other rooms on the first floor, a kitchen, and a small dining room and bathroom.

They moved upstairs and walked down a short corridor to the right and found two small bedrooms and a bathroom. To the left was a larger bedroom and bathroom adjoined.

The Angel turned to the woman who looked exhausted and said, "I think you will be safe here. Why don't you bring your children upstairs and get them into the bedrooms to sleep. You take the larger bedroom for yourself and rest. I will stay downstairs and make sure you are safe."

"I don't know how to thank you. I don't even know who you are."

"I'm sorry. I did forget to introduce myself. I am Branyrd. The LORD sent me here to help you and others find your way."

"I didn't think HE heard my prayers. My husband died and I nearly lost my youngest in the river."

"HE is taking care of your husband but you will need to be strong now and take care of yourself and your children. They need you."

"What is your name?" Branyrd smiled at the woman and placed her hand on her head to calm her.

"I…I…am Myra and my children are Sonya, Caleb and the youngest is Tyler."

"Hmm, devotion to the LORD."

"What did you say, Branyrd?"

"Oh, I noticed your elder son's name means 'faithful or devoted to HIM.'"

"I never thought about that. I liked the name Caleb. My grandfather's name was Caleb."

"Sonya means 'wisdom,'" Branyrd added.

"Oh, I didn't realize that either," Myra stated with a surprised look on her tired face.

"It appears that you were wise in your choice of names for your children."

"What does Tyler mean then?"

"That is another name that is spiritual in meaning, 'influencer to shape things and a sensitive, affectionate and imaginative person.'"

"That is incredible. I did not know any of this. Someone helped me from above, for I had no idea that I was choosing such spiritual names for my children. I hope this fact will keep them safe."

"I don't think you have to worry about that now. Well, I think it is time for you and your children to rest."

"Thank you, Branyrd. I do feel better with you here. Will you stay for a while?"

"Yes, I don't plan on leaving any time soon." Branyrd whispered to herself, after Myra went downstairs to get her children, "At least not until YOU call me home, LORD."

CHAPTER FIVE

Branyrd returned to the living room and looked out one of the windows. She could see many people moving around out there looking confused as they dropped some of their belongings all over the land due to exhaustion.

Benedicto walked into the room and stood there watching Branyrd as she gazed out the window. "Don't worry, Angel. These people cannot see this house. It doesn't really exist."

"What do you mean it doesn't really exist?"

"Well, HE has provided it for temporary shelter until you can find something else for this family."

"What? Oh, right. I remember now. HE has a tendency to do that. I won't worry. I imagine that he will help us find something soon."

"There you go, Angel. I knew you would figure it out on your own," Benedicto chuckled.

"I'm happy to hear that. I have no idea where to take them. But I guess I will figure that out too. HE did say I have a multi-purpose mission to complete. How can I possibly stop all the evil that is around us though?"

"You are not here to stop it but to aid those who are suffering from oppression and help them find their way."

"Their way? Where?"

"Do you remember what you did on your last mission? You found places for everyone in need. You will do that again. For now, let this family rest. I will set the table for then when they awaken. HE has provided some nourishment for them to regain their strength for the journey ahead."

"Thank you, Benedicto."

"Don't thank me, Branyrd. Thank HIM."

"Oh, sorry, yes, thank you, LORD."

Branyrd heard HIS voice in her head. "Do not worry, Angel. I am here for you always. Leave this house after the family is rested and revived with the food. Keep walking until you see a town. There you will find what you need."

"I will, LORD. But what will I find there?"

"Don't worry. You will know when you see it."

"Did you hear that, Benedicto?" Branyrd looked around but didn't see her Guardian Angel. He had performed his disappearing act again.

She left the living room and made her way to the kitchen and dining room. The table was set as Benedicto has said with plenty of food for the whole family. She smelled coffee which made her look for a cup to help herself.

During her previous missions on Earth, Branyrd had become enamored with coffee, chocolate, and ice cream, her three favorite Earth foods. Angels do not need to eat but somehow Branyrd had managed to consume these three items without a problem.

There were plates of chocolate cupcakes, dark chocolate candy and an ice cream scoop nearby but no ice cream. She went to the refrigerator and opened the freezer section. There were a few cartons of chocolate and other flavors of ice cream. She smiled and said a silent 'thank you.'

She sat down to help herself to some dark chocolate candy and a dish of chocolate chunk ice cream. She was so busy eating that she did not hear the pitter patter of little feet coming into the room. What she did hear were screams of delight when the three children spotted all the food.

"Is this for us?" Sonya stepped closer to the table as her siblings rushed to sit down.

"Yes, it is. HE provided it for you. Please sit down and help yourself."

"Do you like chocolate?" Caleb asked the Angel as he stuffed some chicken and mashed potatoes into his mouth.

"Yes, I do. It is one of my favorite things to eat," Branyrd responded with a grin as she watched the children devour all they could.

"I like it too but I am so hungry that I will eat some other things first. I haven't had chicken for a long time," Caleb added.

"That's probably a good idea. Save the cake and candy for last." Branyrd smiled and left the table to allow the children to enjoy themselves as she went upstairs to check on their mother.

Myra was sitting up in bed and looking rested but somewhat confused. "Branyrd, I don't understand why we are here and all the others out there are not."

"I plan to help more soon. I was instructed to help whoever came to me first. You did just that. Come downstairs and have something to eat. Your children are already filling their bellies."

"There is food here?" Myra asked in shock.

"Yes, HE has provided some nourishment for you and your children. We need to leave here soon to travel to another place."

"Where will we go? Will it be safe?"

"Yes, I promise I will find another place for you that is safe."

"How can I ever repay you for all you have done for us. I didn't know what I was going to do when my husband…."

"I understand. You do not have to repay me. I am here to help you."

"Come downstairs, Myra. You can freshen up first in the bathroom."

"Thank you, Branyrd."

Branyrd hurried downstairs when she heard the children talking to someone.

She stopped at the bottom of the stairs and watched Benedicto playing with the children, giving them piggy back rides, at least for the two boys, that is. The girl was a little too grownup to do this, or so she said.

"Branyrd, Come here. This man said he is your friend," Tyler exclaimed with a wide grin as he bounced up and down on the Guardian Angel's back.

"Yes, he is, Tyler. I can see you are having a good time with Benedicto."

"He is funny and so big. We never saw a man this tall before," Caleb called out in excitement.

Sonya giggled and watched from a perch at the table as Benedicto raced around the room with her brothers on his back.

Myra came down the stairs at this moment and stopped in awe. "Who is this man?"

"He is my Guardian Angel, Benedicto. Sorry I didn't introduce him sooner but he was not here at the time," Branyrd explained.

"My children seemed to be having a good time. Is he staying to help us too?"

The boys yelled out loud, "Yes, please come with us, Benedicto!"

Benedicto looked over at Branyrd and winked. "Yes, I will be here if you need me."

CHAPTER SIX

Benedicto cleared the table after everyone had their fill. The food disappeared into thin air along with the house but the children and their mother were already outside with Branyrd and did not see this. It would have been too hard to explain to them otherwise.

Branyrd followed the LORD'S instructions and began walking with the family looking for some sign of a town. There were others all around walking in the same direction now but they could not see her or Benedicto. Once again it would be too difficult to explain who they were and why this huge man and a beautiful woman were walking with them.

The Angel had instructed Myra to keep walking with her children and she and Benedicto would be close behind them.

They had walked for more than an hour before any sign of civilization was spotted. The many people around them rushed forward to the stores, restaurants, and houses that suddenly came into view.

Myra stopped and waited for Branyrd to catch up with her and her children. "What do we do now? There are so many others here."

"I can see that, Myra. Do not worry. I will find a way for everyone to be safe. Stay together though."

Branyrd turned to Benedicto and whispered, "I don't think the shops here will open their doors to all these people. Look at some of the store clerks, they are pushing people away because they are taking things off the shelves and leaving the store. The clerks can't keep up with the onslaught of people.

Benedicto stepped forward, appeared to the people, and stopped them from doing this. Once they saw this large man, they were startled and looked up at him.

One man asked with a frightened voice, "Who are you?"

The Guardian Angel frowned at the man and took the items from him and said, "You cannot take what is not yours."

"I don't have any money and I am hungry," he pleaded.

"I know, but it is still not acceptable. If you need help, you must ask for it."

"I…I have come a long way with my family and don't know what to do. We need food and shelter. Can you help us?"

"Now isn't that better?" Benedicto smiled as he responded.

"Are you going to help us?" the man asked again.

"Yes, I will help all of you. We both will." He looked at Branyrd and called her over.

The others gathered around these two people and waited for them to respond again.

"We will help you. But you must return all the items you took and apologize to the shop owners now," Benedicto explained.

The people who had taken items turned reluctantly and brought the stolen articles back to the shops. The owners came out of the stores and looked shocked to see this happen.

"Who are you?" one owner asked.

Branyrd answered, "We are sent from above to help all of these people find a place to live."

"Why would you help all these people? We don't want them here. They are immigrants and only cause trouble for all of us who live here."

"We need help. We don't know what else to do to survive," one man responded as he bent over in despair.

Branyrd stepped in and said, "You must help by being orderly. That means no stealing. You are here to find a new home, isn't that correct?"

Murmurs of 'yes' could be heard all around. Faces looked confused but expectant of something happening here that could not be explained.

Two men came forward and pulled some of the people away. "Don't listen to this strange man and woman. They mean to harm you."

"We do not mean harm to any of you. If you want a place to live you must come with us. You will need to find jobs and pay your way. We will help you until you can provide for yourselves," Benedicto stated as he watched the look of doubt register on the peoples' faces.

"We have come from many other countries because we couldn't keep our families safe. We heard about this land of freedom and equality where we could live with our families without fear. Is this not true?"

Border guards stepped up behind the crowd and called out to the people, "You must form a line and be processed before you can go into our country."

The two Angels disappeared and waited for the guards to gather the people together and put them on buses to bring to another place for processing.

"These people will be held up for a while. We need to wait to help them after they are processed. HE will provide answers for us. Do not worry, Angel."

Branyrd nodded and sighed. "I see what you mean, Benedicto. We need to wait for them."

Myra and her children looked around for the Angels but did not see them. The children called out for help. "Where are you, Branyrd and Benedicto?"

Benedicto came up to the bus and waved his hands over the kids to calm them down. "I will be with you. Do not worry."

"But we can't see you." Caleb said in an agitated state.

CHAPTER SEVEN

Branyrd and Benedicto flew above the bus and followed it to its destination. They stayed high enough into the clouds so that this bus and the others behind would not see them. It would not be easy to explain to anyone if they were spotted.

The two Angels knew what they had to do once they did leave Earth. They would wave their hands over all the people who had seen them do extraordinary things and erase their memories as they had done on the previous missions. For now, it was all right for others to know that they were Angels but not after they left.

"How many buses do you think are coming this way, Benedicto?" Branyrd asked as she looked through the clouds at the buses below them.

"Too many, Angel," he responded without looking her way.

"It will be difficult to help them all! There are too many!"

"We will do what we can with HIS help as always, Angel. Do not doubt yourself. You are capable of a great many tasks at one time. Have you forgotten what you have accomplished in the past already?"

Branyrd blushed and responded, "Well, sometimes I do and other times I think back at what we have done to help others in need and can't fathom how we did it."

"You know how we did it, Angel." Benedicto met her eye and winked.

"I guess I do – with HIS help as always. We are not alone here. I must keep reminding myself about this."

No sooner were Branyrd's words out of her mouth that she heard a familiar sound – a titter that resounded all around them.

"Did you hear that, Benedicto?" She turned toward her Guardian Angel but he was no longer there.

"Now where did he go?" she asked the air around her.

The buses were slowing down now as they approached a large building. The drivers opened the doors and instructed the people to proceed to the door where a few more Border Guards were stationed and waiting for them.

The people were guided inside the building and told to line up in a single file so that they could be processed.

There were not enough guards to do this work and it appeared to be a long process as each person had to present some form of ID.

Myra and her three children were in the third line that was moving slowly but at least it was moving. They kept looking around them hoping to spot their Angels close behind.

"Mommy, where did the beautiful lady and the big man go? I thought they were coming with us," Caleb asked, always the curious one who asked far too many questions.

"Don't worry. I'm sure they will be coming soon. They probably had to walk all this way. Now try to be quiet. The man will ask us questions. You must all be quiet and let me speak to him. Okay?"

The three children nodded their heads but kept looking behind them for any sign of the Angels.

Myra spoke fluent Spanish and English but her children were not as fluent in English. She would have to make sure that they learned now since they were no longer in their own country.

People kept filing into the building making the space more crowded all the time. The children moved closer to their mother as they got nearer to the front of the line.

Myra stroked her children's heads to calm them down and keep them next to her. The noise level grew as more and more people were inside now.

Tyler held his hands over his ears to block out the noise. He began to cry. "I don't like it here, Mommy! There are too many people and they are talking too loudly. It's taking too long. I want to leave now."

"I know, Tyler. Come here." Myra picked up her youngest and held him close, wiping his tears away. "It will be okay. We will find a place to rest soon."

"Okay, Mommy, but I'm hungry," Tyler exclaimed in between his tears.

"I know, sweet one. We are all hungry and tired. It won't be long now. We are almost at the front of the line."

Branyrd peeked inside the building and spotted the family she was taking care of. She waved at Tyler when he saw her.

"Mommy, the Angels are here!"

When others heard Tyler's words, they too looked around trying to see what the little boy was talking about. They shook their heads and smiled at him when they did not see anyone who looked like they could be an Angel.

Sonya and Caleb waved at Branyrd and tried to run to them but their mother held tightly to their clothes keeping them beside her. She whispered, "Don't move, we are at the head of the line now. Stay here."

Sonya nodded and held onto Caleb's hand until her mother said it was all right to leave and go to Branyrd and Benedicto.

***

There was a scuffle in the back of the line as two men started to argue and throw punches at one another.

Benedicto stepped in between them without being visible and stopped them from fighting, much to their shock. They looked at each other as their punches kept missing. They finally gave up after being too exhausted to keep punching the air between them.

The guards at the door came forward and pulled the two men aside and asked for their papers right away. After a few minutes of perusing their documents, the men were taken away and put back on the waiting buses for anyone who would be deported back to their home country.

"What is going on, Mommy?" Sonya asked as she watched the altercation.

"I don't know, dear. Be quiet now. The man is asking me questions."

Branyrd came alongside the children and calmed them down as the mother finished up with the guard and turned to leave the building. She was told to go back to the bus and wait there for further information.

"Where are we going now, Mommy?" Caleb asked as he turned a frightened face toward Branyrd for help.

Branyrd took his hand and said to the rest, "Come with me."

CHAPTER EIGHT

Branyrd said a silent prayer to the LORD for his instructions where to take the family next. "Where do we go now, LORD? Do I take everyone with us?"

"No, Angel. Just take this family with you for now. I will provide for the others soon."

Branyrd nodded and went in search of Benedicto who appeared behind the first bus. "Here I am, Angel. I have been waiting for you."

"We are to go to the town just over the hill. There is a place we can stay for the night," Branyrd relayed the LORD's instructions to Benedicto.

"Yes, I see it. We should be there in half an hour or so. It is not too difficult a walk for the children. I can carry them if need be."

Tyler was walking next to Benedicto when he stumbled on a rock. He bent down to rub his sore knee and began to cry. "Mommy, my knee is bleeding."

Branyrd looked at Tyler's knee and said, "Look it stopped bleeding now. It is almost better already."

Tyler nodded and smiled in relief. Turning to his mother he asked, "Can you carry me, Mommy?"

Before his mother could pick him up, Tyler was transported on top of Benedicto's shoulder much to his delight. He let out a cry of wonder being up so high in the air.

"Look at me, Mommy! I am flying! I can almost touch the sky!"

"Can you pick me up too, Benedicto?" Caleb asked, clearly envious of his brother's sky-view perch.

Before he knew it, Caleb was beside his brother on Benedicto's right shoulder. Both boys held onto Benedicto's shirt and his head to keep from falling.

Sonya smiled up at them when they called down to her to join them. "I am fine down here. There is no room for me either."

Benedicto smiled at her and winked. "Are you sure, little lady?"

"Yep, I'm sure. I like being right here. Thank you though, Benedicto."

The boys had forgotten how tired, hungry, and frightened they had been previously in the large building and now were enjoying the view from their high perch.

Myra walked next to Branyrd so she could talk to her. "Where are you taking us?"

"You will see soon. We will be there shortly."

"I don't understand why you are taking care of only us. There are so many others in need also."

"Yes, there are many in need. We will take care of them soon enough. Right now, we will find a place for you to stay more permanently than the previous one. You will need to get settled and then within a year you must file a form to seek asylum. Then you will have to find a job and get the children into a school as soon as you get your green card for asylum.

"The guard gave me a card with a date on it to apply." Myra showed Branyrd her card. "Does this mean we can stay here?"

"It looks that way but you must not forget to fill out the necessary paperwork. If you need help, I can assist you."

"Yes, I think I would like that. I don't know what I am doing. My husband, Neville, had all the information and he is gone now. Thank goodness I held onto our paperwork or that would be lost along with him." Myra cried as she held her head in her hands and stopped moving.

Branyrd gathered the bereft woman into her arms and held her, giving her much needed strength and comfort.

Myra stepped away reluctantly and nodded to Branyrd her thanks. "You have done so much for us already; I can never fully repay you for your kindness."

"You do not need to repay me, Myra, just be strong for your children and never give up. Remember, you are not alone. Neville is watching over you along with the LORD."

"Thank you, Branyrd. I hope he is proud of us that we are doing our best to survive without him. I miss him so terribly though. I never expected to lose him like that. We came all this way and then…"

"I know. It is a difficult road you are traveling, Myra. That is why we are here to aid you in any way we can. There are many others with similar stories like yours who have also suffered losses too terrible to comprehend."

'I'm sorry for complaining like this, Branyrd. I can't let my children see weakness in me. They need to learn to be strong like their father was. I will learn that too."

"Yes, you will grow stronger with each day, don't worry. I am here until you are settled. Okay?"

"I appreciate that. But what will we do after you leave us?"

"HE will always be there for you. All you have to do is pray to HIM."

"I have been praying all the way to our new land. Maybe that is why you are here now. HE heard me."

***

There were many people coming up behind them who were also allowed to leave the building. They were looking for places to stay and pushing and shoving their way through as they got closer to the Angels.

Benedicto turned toward them and put up his hands to them. "You must not push and shove others. We are all trying to find a safe place. If you need help, ask HIM."

"Who?" one confused man asked in broken English.

"Who do we ask?" another person responded.

The Guardian Angel smiled and waved his hands over the agitated people to calm them and then responded in their own languages all at once.

"You will know who to ask because HE is always there for all of you. If you cannot pray, you will find it more difficult to find help."

"We have been praying every day in our own religion for help but no one has answered our prayers."

"Are you sure about that?" Benedicto asked as he watched the wide-eyed expressions on their faces over his words.

CHAPTER NINE

The small town came into view as the tired travelers sighed in relief. Benedicto helped the children down from his shoulders. The boys ran ahead to look around the town with their sister close behind keeping an eye on them.

Many other people followed behind them and spread out over the town looking for places to eat and sleep. A few stores closed and locked their doors when they spotted the crowd heading into town. The owners did not know if they could trust the mob to be orderly.

Benedicto stepped forward and knocked on the door of a restaurant that had locked their doors and put out a closed sign. The manager came to the door and peeked out at the giant man.

"What do you want?"

The Guardian Angel smiled and waved his hands over the man to calm him. "I am not here to harm you nor are any of the others. They just need a place to eat and rest. Could you please open your doors so that they can have something. They have traveled far and are hungry and thirsty. I assure you they will not cause any trouble. I am here to make sure they don't."

"How do I know that? Who are you anyway?" the man asked as he gazed up at the giant of a man.

"I was sent here to help these people by HIM."

"HIM? Who is that?"

"Do you believe in a place greater than this?"

"What do you mean?" the man asked in confusion.

"Heaven. Do you believe in Heaven?"

"Well, I guess I do. My wife believes."

As the man fumbled through the conversation, his wife came forward to join him. She listened to the man mention Heaven. "Yes, I believe in Heaven. There has to be a place better than this. Look at all these people. They keep coming here. Do they think that this is Heaven?"

"Maybe this is a better place than where they came. To them this must feel close to being like Heaven," Benedicto explained.

"I see. What happened to them to cause them to come here?" the woman asked.

"There are many reasons why they come to your town. They want to be free, safe and away from the harm that they have suffered at the hands of others in their countries."

"Oh, the children do look hungry and tired." Turning to her husband the woman pleaded, "Honey, we must let them in. Look at the children. Some of them are hurt."

The man gazed out at the crowd who were standing around and looking exhausted. He saw the bruises and scrapes on the children's knees. He felt his heart opening to them. He reached for the sign and turned it over and opened the door wider.

Benedicto smiled at the couple and said, "Thank you. You will be rewarded by HIM. HE is pleased by your generosity and kindness."

"What?" the woman exclaimed. "What did you say?"

"HE is pleased with you," Benedicto repeated.

"Is HE here now?" she asked, looking around.

"HE is always here," Benedicto explained, touching his chest.

"Wait a minute, will these people pay their way if I let them in?" the man asked, looking at them warily,

"I assure you they will," the Guardian Angel replied.

"Okay then. The man called out to the people, "Come in and find a seat. We will take care of you as soon as we can."

The people scrambled through the door trying not to crowd each other. Benedicto stopped them and let only a few in at a time in order to prevent chaos.

The man nodded in appreciation and hurried into the kitchen to prepare for the onslaught of orders. He called out to his waiters to get out to the tables and begin taking orders.

His wife assisted the people to tables and made room for as many as she could. There were still too many to fit inside at one time.

Benedicto and Branyrd spoke to the others who were anxiously waiting to enter. "You will have to wait your turn. There is not enough room for all of you."

Branyrd whispered to Benedicto, "What if we help them find room? We can set up some tables outside for the others."

"Sounds like a good idea. We can help wait on tables to hurry up the process. Maybe you can go into the kitchen and cook, Angel," Benedicto quipped as he laughed at the face Branyrd made back at him.

"You know I can't cook, Benedicto."

"You could if you asked HIM for help."

"I will not bother HIM with such trivial matters. I will help with the tables and bring food to the people."

"That would work too, Angel." Benedicto pulled tables and chairs out of the air and set them up on the sidewalk. The people came forward to claim a seat as they looked on in wonder about how the tables had appeared.

Branyrd took water to all the people inside and out of the restaurant so that they could wash their hands and faces as they waited for their food.

Inside the restaurant the pace was frantic as the waiters took orders, rushed to the kitchen to fulfill them. They rushed back as orders were completed then delivered them to the hungry crowd.

Branyrd lent a hand as she picked up the orders that had to be delivered to the people outside. Once everyone was sated, they were relaxed and no longer agitated.

The time came to pay their bills and the people shook their heads. Benedicto raced inside and took the waiters aside to explain. "These people do not understand you and do not have any money to pay for their meals. I will take care of all of them."

Branyrd looked at Benedicto in surprise. "You have money?"

"No, not exactly but I have something better. Go look in the kitchen.

Branyrd disappeared and came back with her eyes wide.

Inside the kitchen the couple were speechless. All around them were baskets and baskets of all kinds of food. In fact, there was more food than they had just cooked for the people, enough to last them for a long time.

The man and woman came out to thank the giant man and the beautiful lady but they were no longer there.

CHAPTER TEN

The people slowly got up from the tables and left the restaurant. They thanked the waiters for the food in their own languages and some in broken English. They bowed and kissed the cheeks of surprised waiters who didn't know how to respond but tears could be seen in their eyes.

The owners stood looking out at the people as they moved away from their restaurant. There was still no sign of the two people who were there with them.

The woman turned to her husband with tears in her eyes, "Do you think that they were Angels?"

"Maybe. I don't know what to say. How could all that food get here? We never saw anyone bring it in."

"Yes, I believe they were Angels, dear," the woman responded and smiled as she looked up and whispered, "thank you."

***

Benedicto and Branyrd were looking around for a place for everyone to stay. No one wanted to let the people into the hotel or the private homes.

"I think we are going to need HIS assistance again, Benedicto."

"Let's see what we can do first. We do have powers, Angel, never forget that."

"I guess we will have to build a hotel?"

"No, I don't think we will need to do that yet."

"Let's think about this. These people need a place to rest, some shelter over their heads," Branyrd mused.

Branyrd looked around at the small town. There wasn't much to offer for so many.

"Come with me, Angel."

Branyrd followed Benedicto into a field. "This will be perfect for them."

"I don't understand. There are no buildings here."

"We will put some tents up for them until we can find a more permanent place."

49

"I will take the mother and her three children to that house over there. It is not occupied. It has a for sale sign on it."

"Yes, I think that is the one HE wanted you to take them to."

Branyrd looked around for her four charges and found them wandering around the town. She called out to them, "Come with me, Myra. I found a place for you and your children."

Myra perked up when she heard Branyrd's voice. "I didn't know where you had gone. I thought it was time for you to leave us."

"Not yet, Myra. This is the house where you will be staying with your children. I will take care of the sale and get the key. Wait here."

Branyrd disappeared and came back shortly with a key and some paperwork.

"How did you do that? You just disappeared right in front of us."

"HE did that. Here is your paperwork for the house. All you need to do is sign it all. I will bring it back to the real estate office. It is now yours. You can take down the for-sale sign and move in."

"We don't have anything to move in, just us."

Branyrd opened the door and led the astonished family inside their new home. Everything was inside – furniture in all rooms, food in the kitchen, and clothes in the four bedrooms.

"But how did you do all this? I don't understand." Myra wiped tears out of her eyes as she wandered from room to room as the children raced upstairs to check out their bedrooms.

"HE did all this. You need only to take care of yourself and your children and thank HIM that way. HE will be watching over you."

"I don't know what to say or how to thank you, Branyrd."

"You already have. Take care, Myra. I will be close by if you need me. For now, I must assist the others."

When Branyrd went back to the field, Benedicto was setting up tents with beds, pillows, and blankets. He was ushering people into the tents to get settled.

Two men were arguing outside a tent about who would be staying there. "This is my tent. Find your own!" one man yelled to the other.

One man stepped forward and punched another man resulting in more fighting and squabbling about where they would sleep.

Benedicto stepped between the men and called out in a voice that hurt their ears, "Stop what you are doing now!"

The startled men looked up at him and shivered in fear. "What do you want us to do?" one asked.

"I want you to find a tent and get inside without fighting. There is no need to fight. There are plenty of tents for everyone."

"Okay," one man cried out as he pushed another aside to get in the tent where his family were now settled.

When all were settled inside tents, Benedicto and Branyrd looked around the town to find other places that could be used for the immigrants.

Outside the town there were others who were watching what was going on. These individuals pulled out their guns and waited for the cover of darkness before venturing forward.

CHAPTER ELEVEN

Branyrd heard the LORD's voice in her head. "Good job, Angel. Be alert, there is danger close by. I will be watching over you."

"I don't see anything, LORD. What are we to do now?"

"You will know when it is time."

Benedicto was watching over the sleeping people as he walked back and forth around the outside of the field. He could feel the anger and evil nearby.

Branyrd alerted Benedicto about what the LORD had told her. "There will be trouble."

"Yes, I can feel it. Open your arms and you will feel it too."

"I can. It is evil. We need to protect these people."

"We will. I need to move out into the wooded area there. Wait here and stay alert."

"Do you need me to come with you?"

"No, you are better off here to watch over these people. We will have more work to do tomorrow when they awaken."

"I can imagine we will. Call me if you need me."

"Keep your mind open to me and I will."

"It is always open to you, Benedicto," Branyrd guffawed as she watched him fly over the woods without a sound.

What Branyrd didn't know yet was that there were many more dangerous individuals coming their way who could cause harm to many.

***

The influx continued with many thousands coming across borders all over the countries on Earth. There were too many to handle for the towns and cities who would receive the onslaught.

In some places the towns suffered from marauding and killing of innocent people who tried to stop them. Police tried in vain to curtail the flow but there was not enough law enforcement to do that.

The LORD watched as the people were uncontrollable. HE needed to send the Angels this way. HE could hear whispers of prayers being said as those who suffered were unable to protect themselves, their families, and their homes from the prowlers.

Branyrd heard the cries as the LORD opened a window for her to see what was happening all over the Earth.

"Do you need us to go there now, LORD?"

"Soon, Angel. Wait until I call you."

"Yes, LORD. But Benedicto is not here. I need to wait for him to return."

HIS voice was silent as Branyrd waited for her Guardian Angel to return. It had been a long time, too long since Benedicto had flown away. "What is he doing?" she asked out loud to no one.

Benedicto watched the men in the woods creeping closer to the tents. He snapped a tree and it fell over in front of the men preventing them from moving forward.

"Did you see that?" one man cried out in alarm.

"Ssh, be quiet, you idiot. They will hear us. It was just a tree."

"But it fell in front of us. How did that happen?"

"I don't know. Do I look like a lumberjack?"

"Well, how do you explain it? Don't call me an idiot!"

"You are an idiot. I don't know why I took you along with me. I should have left you behind for the guards to capture."

"If you did, then you would not have enough men to do whatever you plan to do."

"There are many more coming this way. Don't worry about that. You better shut your trap or you will not be able to speak again once I finish with you."

The frightened man stayed silent. He knew that this man wasn't kidding. He moved along behind several other armed men but stopped when he heard something overhead. What he saw was too difficult to explain.

He poked the man in front of him and pointed upwards. The man poked him back and told him to be quiet.

"But I saw something up there," he tried to explain.

"What did you see," the other man whispered.

"I don't know how to explain what I saw. You probably won't believe me anyway," he sighed as he looked upward again but nothing was there.

The other man looked up at the same time. "I don't see anything."

"There was something there, I swear. It had large white wings and…."

"What? Are you crazy?"

"No, I saw it. I know I did."

"No wonder Amir calls you an idiot!"

The man shook his head and rubbed his eyes to try and clear his vision. Maybe he did imagine what he saw. No one will believe me anyway, he thought. He stayed quiet as they kept moving along toward the tents.

CHAPTER TWELVE

Benedicto flew back to Branyrd with a warning. "There are several men coming through the woods with guns. They plan to kill all these people who did not pay them for bringing them here."

"Did they say that?"

"No, but I read their minds. They are traffickers, dealing in humans of all ages."

"Do you mean that is how all these people came here with these traffickers? Where would these poor people get money if they came with just the clothes on their backs?" Branyrd was perplexed.

"That is a good question, Angel. They probably promised to pay the men as soon as they arrived here."

"I'm surprised that these men would even bring them here if they had not received payment in full beforehand."

"That would make sense. But evidently the people ran away from the men before they could say that they didn't have the money."

Branyrd silently prayed for an answer.

"Yes, that is what we must do now!" Benedicto began his own prayers for help.

The LORD was watching and heard their prayers. HE sent down a bolt of lightning along with a shower of rain that kept the men from moving any further.

Branyrd and Benedicto were instructed to fly over the men and push them back to the river.

When the men looked up through the rain they saw two large figures with wings. The man who had already spotted Benedicto pointed and exclaimed, "See, I told you! That is what I saw before!"

The Angels sent thoughts to the leader's mind to turn around and leave now.

Amir yelled out to his men, "Turn around now and get back to the river. We don't need this money that much."

To ensure that the men didn't change their minds, the Angels sent along sparks at their heels to frighten them from coming back.

"They will not return, Benedicto."

"No, I don't think they will."

"We can thank HIM for that storm. We better get back to the tents to make sure the people are okay," Branyrd said, as she sighed in relief.

"They should be fine. I don't think they even heard the storm."

"They are probably too exhausted to even care at this point. With full stomachs they must have slept through it."

Branyrd relayed what the LORD showed her in the window. "We may have to leave to help others soon."

"I can imagine there are many more poor souls in need. We must do what we can to help these and then go where HE tells us."

"We can look around for more places for these people to get settled until morning."

"Yes, I think we need to do that, Angel. You go in that direction and I will go this way. There are bound to be more buildings that are deserted or for sale."

The Angels searched the town and beyond until the first light of day. They had found a large office building that was in poor condition. With some work it could be suitable for many of the immigrants to stay. It was time to get the people proactive in this mission.

Many of the people came out of the tents and looked around. They stretched and yawned and walked around to see what others were going to do. They looked for the large man and the beautiful lady but they were nowhere in sight.

One man announced, "I heard lightning close by last night. Did you hear it? It smells like it rained but the ground around us is dry."

A woman replied, "I didn't hear anything. I slept well for once with a full belly."

"Me too," another person reiterated.

"Where are the two people who helped us? Has anyone seen them?" one man, who was taking on the job of leader, asked.

There were several negative murmurs. The people spread out in different directions to find their benefactors.

The Angels were flying around the building that they had found and were putting some touches to it to prepare it for the people. They wanted the people to work to do the rest of it though. They flew as close as they could without anyone seeing them and walked the rest of the way to the people who were gathered in the street.

"There you are!" the man who was now the leader, exclaimed.

"Yes, we are here. We have been busy looking for a place for all of you to stay but we need your help. Are any of you proficient in building, carpentry or handy that way?" Benedicto asked.

Many men raised their hands and stepped forward. "What can we do to help you?" the leader asked.

"Come with us," Branyrd instructed. "We have jobs for all of you if you want to have a safe place to get settled."

A chorus of 'yes' was heard all around. The men and women with children close behind followed the two people to see what they had to do.

When the people spotted the derelict building, they moaned as one. The leader asked, "How are we going to fix this place? It's a mess!"

Branyrd stepped forward. "Yes, it is now but you are going to fix it and make it habitable for all of you. You better get started. You have a big job to complete. Those tents cannot stay there. The town will not allow them to be there for long."

"Where are we going to get tools and wood to do this?" one man asked as he shook his head at the prospect of this enormous task.

"Look inside. You will find everything you need to complete the project. We will provide whatever else you need."

The leader led the way and stopped short when he saw all the tools and other equipment that was necessary to complete this renovation. He began to get excited and directed the rest of the men to get working on fixing the walls and making them sturdy with the supplies that were available.

Each man took up a task and began working with vigor. They felt energized to do these jobs for not only themselves, but also their families.

The Angels stepped aside and watched with wide grins. "I think we can leave now, Branyrd. It looks like they have everything they need to live safely here."

"I better check on Myra and her children to see if they need anything else before we move on," Branyrd announced, not looking too happy to leave.

When Branyrd got back to the house where Myra was now owner she stopped and prepared herself to tell them that she was leaving.

CHAPTER THIRTEEN

Myra came to the door and welcomed Branyrd in. "Please come in, Branyrd. Would you like some breakfast?"

"No, I am not hungry but I would like a cup of coffee if you made it."

"Of course. Please sit down." The Angel sipped the hot coffee that was placed in front of her and sighed.

The children heard her voice and came running over. "You are back! We missed you."

"Branyrd," the Angel reminded them.

"Hi Branyrd. We love our new house and our own bedrooms. I never had my own bedroom," Sonya announced, beaming.

"Yes, me too," Caleb chirped in.

"What about you, Tyler? Are you happy with your room too?"

"Yep, I like my room too, but it is the smallest. I guess because I am the smallest," he chuckled.

"That means it is just right for you, Tyler," Branyrd responded.

"Why are you sad, Branyrd?" Tyler asked as he looked at her face that was shown with a golden light behind her head that was not as bright as before.

"That is why I am here to see you all. I must leave now to help others in need. HE has asked me to go. I really don't want to leave you so soon but there are so many others in need."

"Oh no, Branyrd! You can't leave us yet!" the children exclaimed in unison.

"I'm sorry. But you are safe here now and have everything you need. If you need anything else before I leave, please let me know."

"No, we only need you," Tyler cried, tears dripped from his chin as he looked at the Angel.

"Please don't cry, Tyler. You will make me cry too. I promise to watch over you. I hope you will always remember me."

"I will, I promise!" he said through his tears.

"We will too, Branyrd," Sonya and Caleb added.

"Well, then I guess it is time for me to go. Listen to your mother, help her, and work hard in school."

"Okay, we promise," Sonya said with tears in her eyes.

The children came up to Branyrd and gave her tight hugs and didn't want to let go. Myra wrapped Branyrd in a warm hug also and said, "Thank you so much for all your help. We couldn't have done this without you. I hope we will see you again."

"I don't know if I will be back but I will certainly keep watch over you all as long as HE allows me to. Take care. It was a pleasure to meet you all."

"We love you, Branyrd!" the children called out to her as she moved toward the door.

"I love you too!" the Angel said through tears that threatened to fall.

Benedicto was outside waiting for her. "I would like to see the people working one last time. I want them to know that we will be watching them and sending our love to them too."

"Branyrd, you are being a human again. Dry your eyes and let's say our last goodbyes. They will be all right now. Don't worry so much. HE is taking care of them."

"I know. I can't help myself. I worry about everyone and everything when I am on Earth."

The men were busy moving from room to room and shoring up the walls. They looked down at the Angels who were waiting to say something to them.

"Do you need to tell us something?" the leader asked, puzzled at the expressions on the faces of their two saviors.

Branyrd wiped her eyes and responded, "We are leaving now and wanted to make sure you are doing well without our help. Is there anything you need before we go?"

"You have done so much to help us. We can't repay you. All we can do is say, thank you from the bottom of our hearts."

Others came forward and gripped the Angels hands in warm handshakes and pats on their backs in gratitude.

Behind them there were many townsmen coming forward to lend a hand to the workers. The two Angels stepped aside to let them by. One of the men was the owner of the restaurant. He came up to the Angels and shook hands with them.

"I am glad you are here. I wanted to thank you for what you did for us with all the food. How you did that and why I will never comprehend. My wife said that you are Angels. Maybe she is right. I just don't know. But whatever, I believe you were sent by HIM for sure."

Branyrd and Benedicto nodded and smiled. "It was our pleasure to help you. It was our mission to give hope to all of you. Work together and get along, that is all we ask in return."

"We plan to do that. My wife is making sandwiches and will be coming soon to feed all these people. We have more than enough food available, thanks to you. No matter how much we use there is always more. That is quite perplexing but we are thankful for the bounty."

"We must leave now. There are others who need our help."

"I'm sorry you are leaving. You will be missed. My wife will be sad that she missed you."

"We will stop by your restaurant and say goodbye to her."

"She will be happy you did. Thank you again." The man bowed to them and went into the building to lend a hand along with many other townspeople.

After the Angels left the restaurant and shared hugs with the woman there, Branyrd wiped her eyes once again and sighed, "I hate to leave everyone here, Benedicto. I don't know what we will find next. There are so many in need."

"Yes, there are far too many. We will do what we can for the next part of your mission. No worries. HE will help you along the way and so will I."

Branyrd smiled and nodded through her tears that refused to stop. She looked up to Heaven and whispered a silent prayer to help her do whatever HE needed her to do next.

CHAPTER FOURTEEN

The Angels were silently whisked away to the next part of the mission. They arrived in a town that was on fire. People were running in all directions as fire trucks and police were trying to control the chaos around them.

Branyrd looked around her. "What is happening here, LORD?"

She heard HIS voice in her head. "This is the next part of your mission, Angel. You need to control the chaos and get the people out of harm's way."

"I will do my best." She looked right and left and saw children injured and lying in the street. She went to them first and lifted them up. She ran her hands over their injuries and calmed their fears when they opened their eyes and saw her.

The parents were nearby and also injured. Benedicto aided Branyrd and healed the parents enabling them to take charge of their children and get to safety.

"Who are you?" one mother asked as she picked up her child and held him close.

"We are here to help you. HE heard your prayers and sent us here."

"I did pray but didn't think that anyone heard me. Thank you."

"Don't thank us, thank HIM."

"I will. I promise. Where are we to go now? Our house is on fire along with our business. Those men took everything before they started the fire. Now we have nothing."

"Keep praying to HIM. HE will find a way for you."

Branyrd looked up and prayed for a way to help them along with so many others that were floundering in front of them.

She heard HIS voice. "Take them to the City Hall, Angel. There they will find a place to stay for now. You have much more to do."

Branyrd led the people that were in the street as she was instructed by the LORD. Once they were all there, she asked for help from the city officials.

"These people need a place to stay now that their houses are destroyed. What can you do for them?"

Some just shook their heads while others walked away without responding. The only ones that came forward were the people in the van with a cross on it. It was a first aid truck that was taking care of the injured.

A kindly woman took the people from Branyrd and said, "We will find a place for them. We will set up a tent to treat and feed them until we can find some other places to house them."

"Thank you," Branyrd said as she took the woman's hand and blessed her.

The woman felt a shock at Branyrd's touch and said, "What did you do to me?"

"I blessed you for your kindness. HE is here to watch over you."

"Who are you and who is HE?" she asked in confusion.

"We were sent here by HIM to help you and others."

"I don't understand."

"Do you believe in the LORD? In Heaven?"

"Well, of course I do. I was taught by a preacher father and brought up in a religious family setting."

"Then you will know what to do when HE calls you."

"Will HE call me? I am a lowly sinner. I am not worthy."

"But you are more than worthy for what you are doing here to help others."

"What is your name?" Branyrd inquired.

"I am Hannah. Who are you?"

"My name is Branyrd and this is Benedicto. We are here on a Mission of Hope."

"Hmm, I see. Does that mean that you are Angels?"

"I guess you can say that," Branyrd snickered.

Hannah bowed to them and fell to her knees. "I never thought that I would ever see an Angel on Earth, never mind in Heaven. I do hope to get there one day."

"Please don't bow to us, only to HIM. I don't think you will have any problem getting to Heaven one day, Hannah. I think HE has a place for you already."

"Do you mean I am going to die soon?" Hannah asked in horror.

"Oh no, I do not mean that nor do I know when that will be. Sorry to frighten you. Death is not meant to be frightening. HE will pave a way for you when HE is ready. I do not know anything about that."

"Well, I had better get working harder. These people need me now."

"Yes, they do," Branyrd said as she waved goodbye to Hannah and the people who were waving back in gratitude.

Branyrd watched as the fires were slowly extinguished by the firemen but the police were still searching for those responsible for the destruction. She followed them from a high perch above the city.

She spotted many men who were gathered in a park with several items in their hands. She landed in front of their astonished faces.

"What? Who are you?" one surprised man asked.

"I see that you have things that do not belong to you." Branyrd asked, ignoring his question.

"Who are you?" another man asked in a stronger voice.

"I am Branyrd. HE has sent me here."

"What kind of name is that?" another asked, guffawing rudely.

"Who is HE? Is this another gang member?" another younger man asked in a shaky voice.

"No, stupid. We are the gang to be feared. She is no one," the leader announced, showing bravado.

"You need to return these items to City Hall and turn yourselves in."

"What are you, crazy? These are ours!"

"You cannot take what is not yours, for HE knows."

"There you go again with HE. Who is this person you keep mentioning?" the gang leader asked again.

"HE is the LORD who you must obey and atone for your sins."

"Haha, now I've heard everything! You've got to be kidding! Don't get in our way or you will be sorry," the leader warned as he stepped closer to Branyrd.

CHAPTER FIFTEEN

What happened next was not to be expected by the gang. A brilliant light came down from the sky and landed in front of the gang leader who jumped back in alarm.

The light singed the man's shoes and caused them to catch fire. The man jumped up and down trying to put the fire out. He yelled to his gang members for help, "Someone help me! Put out the fire!"

The members stood there in shock and couldn't move as their leader jumped around helplessly in pain until Branyrd raised her hands over his feet and stopped the flames.

This caused all the gang to step back even further as they waited for what would transpire in front of them next.

"How did you do that?" one tremulous man asked.

"I did not do anything. It was HE."

"Who is this person that you keep talking about?" the leader finally asked once he could get his voice back. He was still visibly shaking.

"You need to change your ways or more things will happen to you. Do you understand?" Branyrd stared at the men with lightning in her eyes.

"Please do not hurt us." the men said as they backed away in fear.

"I will not harm you but HE may if you do not stop this violence and destruction of property. Do you understand?"

The gang was silent and waited for their leader to say something.

"I understand that you did some hocus pocus stuff on me to scare us. I don't believe anything you have to say or do."

Turning to his men he said, "Come on. Let's get out of here. We need to sell this stuff."

Before the leader could move more than an inch, he was struck again by a bolt of lightning but this time he fell to his death.

The men around him ran away and dropped all the stolen goods at Branyrd's feet. The Angel gathered the items and flew back to the people who were surprised by her return with their property.

Branyrd met Hannah and explained what she had in her possession and why. Hannah took the items and distributed them to their owners who waved in thanks for Branyrd. They piled the items next to them and planned to keep them with them until they found a place to stay.

Benedicto in the meantime had picked up the gang members and brought them to the police station to be kept in jail until they could be prosecuted.

The police were surprised to see a large man pushing a group of startled gang members into the station. They stood aside as Benedicto explained what the men had done.

"They are all yours, gentlemen. I am sure they will share more about what they did and why. I take my leave."

Benedicto backed out leaving everyone questioning what just happened and why.

The Guardian Angel returned to Branyrd's side to relay that the men wouldn't be back. "The police will take care of them now."

"That's a relief. It was unfortunate that the leader did not listen. I don't want to see anyone die like that."

"Well, evidently HE had other plans for him to start repaying his way."

"I understand but it is still difficult to see. I pray that all these people will find peace soon."

"That is part of your mission, Angel. You are to help them."

"There are more over there, Benedicto." Branyrd pointed to the crowd that was gathered at the end of the street.

The Angels flew high above the crowd to see what was happening.

"It looks like there is more trouble for the police," Branyrd said as she pointed to the men with repeaters.

"I think we better go down and investigate," Benedicto suggested as he waited for Branyrd to agree.

Branyrd stated, "Most definitely. There will be trouble."

As they landed behind the men with the guns, the crowd gasped at the sight of the Angels' landing.

The men quickly turned around to see what the people were pointing to.

Branyrd raised her hands to the men and heated the guns, forcing them to drop them.

"What? Who are you? How did you do that?" one man asked in agitation, as he blew on his hands.

"What are you doing here?" Branyrd asked.

"We are taking what is ours," one man said as he stepped closer to the Angel.

Benedicto grinned at the man and said, "I wouldn't go too close if I were you."

Branyrd raised one hand this time and stopped the man in his tracks as he tried to move. His feet were stuck like glue on the tar.

"What did you do to me?" he asked in horror.

"I would suggest that you and the rest of your men leave this area now or you will be brought to the police station like the others."

"What others?" he queried.

"Who are you?" another man asked but kept his distance.

"I am Branyrd and this is Benedicto. We were sent here to help those in need. You do not look like you are in need."

"How do you know that? We are in need," the men insisted.

"What do you need?" Branyrd asked.

"Well, um...we...um." The man turned to the other men and pleaded with them. "Help me here."

"You are on your own, man. We are out of here." The men turned and ran in the opposite direction.

The people who were being held at gunpoint clapped in response.

"Thank you," they all called out to the Angels.

"Whoever you are, we are thankful," one man responded as he shook the Angels' hands.

One woman asked, "Is it true you were sent here to help us?"

"Yes, HE sent us. Many of you have been praying and your prayers have been heard."

The people bowed and said, "You have to be Heaven sent. Who else could have done what you just did?"

"What do you need for us to do for you? Do you have places to go to be safe?" Branyrd asked.

One woman responded, "Most of us have lost our homes from this fire thanks to those men and others. We have nowhere to go."

Branyrd touched each person on their hands and said, "You will come with us. We will find you a place that is safe."

The Angels led these people to Hannah who was busy feeding the growing number of people that the Angels kept bringing her.

Hannah looked up and saw the Angels heading her way with many others in tow. All she could do was sigh and say a prayer for help.

Branyrd went over to the van where the food was being prepared and waved her hands as instructed by the LORD to replenish the supplies. She next turned to the tents and did the same there, increasing the number of tents for the addition of more people.

When Hannah saw what Branyrd had done she cried. "I didn't believe you at first that you were Angels. But now there is no doubt. I am sorry for doubting you."

"No worries, Hannah. I still find it hard to believe that I can do these things with HIS help too. There is no end to what we can accomplish with HIS help. Always remember that."

Benedicto sniggered at Branyrd's words. "I see you are remembering these things now yourself, Angel."

"Yes, I am finally, Benedicto. It's about time, isn't it?" she smiled back at him.

Shouting could be heard in the distance causing the Angels to flee in a hurry away from the group to see what was happening.

CHAPTER SIXTEEN

A car raced by with guns shooting in all directions. People scattered and took cover.

The Angels flew over to prepare a barrier to protect anyone in the way of the bullets. One innocent child was not so lucky as he lay on the sidewalk bleeding from a wound as his parents tried to staunch the flow of blood with their hands.

Branyrd went to their aid and held her hands over the child's body as the parents watched in awe. The blood stopped gushing out and the wound appeared to be healing in front of their eyes.

"How did you do that?" the mother asked in wonder.

"However you did that, we are grateful beyond measure," the father said through his tears.

"I did not do that. It was HE."

"Who?" the father asked.

"The LORD is the one who healed your son. HE heard your prayers."

"I don't know what to say. Who are you?" the mother asked.

"I am known as Branyrd. This is Benedicto. We were sent here in answer to all the prayers that HE has been receiving."

"You mean, GOD has sent you? Then you must be HIS Angels," the father sighed and bowed before them.

"Yes, we are his messengers. There is no need to bow before us. Only bow before the LORD," Branyrd responded.

"Thank you, GOD!" the parents cried out.

Benedicto smiled and gathered the men who were responsible for shooting the boy and brought them to the jail. As before, the police stood there with their mouths ajar and did not know what to say but nodded in thanks to the giant of a man.

The officers mumbled and looked shocked at the growing number of people who were brought in by this stranger. They had so many questions but this giant never stayed long enough to answer them.

All they could do was bring the men to the jail cells until they could interrogate each one to find out why they were there.

In the meantime, Branyrd led the new group of people to Hannah to feed and house in the tents. The area was now full of people who were waiting to get something to eat and a place to rest.

The LORD instructed the Angels to go to the courthouse right away. Branyrd flew around with Benedicto to find the courthouse. When they arrived, they found the court in session with a man who was suspected of killing a man and a woman in cold blood.

They listened at the back of the courtroom to the evidence on both sides and waited to hear what the judge had to say.

Branyrd heard the defendant's thoughts and shook her head. "The judge cannot find this man innocent. We need to fix this, Benedicto." But her Guardian Angel was nowhere in sight.

The Angel flew over to the judge under cover and bent down to whisper in his ear.

The judge's face looked shocked and whipped his head around to see who had just spoken to him. There was no one nearby but he cleared his throat and began to speak to the courtroom, "The defendant will stand to hear my verdict."

The man stood and waited as he wore a smirk on his face when he met his lawyer's eye. This smirk soon turned to horror as he heard what the judge had to say.

"You have committed a heinous crime of murder and will be sentenced to twenty years in prison. Court is dismissed. Take him away."

Branyrd smiled and swiftly flew out of the courthouse to find Benedicto.

"Where have you been?" she asked him as he stood outside the courthouse as if he had all the time in the world to rest.

She relayed what the verdict was. "I think the judge felt that he needed to give a message to all who break the law."

"Well, I think you may have somehow convinced him to feel that way, right, Angel?" he replied with a smile.

"Maybe a little bit. I couldn't see how he would find this man or anyone else innocent who had committed such a crime."

"I think he will be quite busy over the next month or so with all the cases that are waiting for him," Benedicto added.

"Hopefully he will put them all away and not let them on the street again to harm someone else. That appears to be what is happening here," Branyrd said with a heavy sigh.

"That is why we are here, Angel, to make sure that all who have harmed their fellow man will be incarcerated to keep them away from others until HE can call them home for penance."

"By the looks of things, Benedicto, the jails and prisons will soon be full of these perpetrators. We need to help turn them around from their evil ways. Maybe that is what HE wants us to do."

"How do you plan to do that, Branyrd?" Benedicto queried as he raised his brows in a quirky way.

"Oh, Benedicto. You look so strange when you do that," Branyrd giggled. "I will find a way."

"I bet you will," he responded as he once again disappeared.

"Now where did you go?" Branyrd asked as she sighed with a smile.

CHAPTER SEVENTEEN

Branyrd flew back to the crowd that was being tended to by Hannah to make sure that she didn't need any additional help. While she was there, Branyrd restocked the supply of food, tents, and other necessary items with help from HIM.

Once that was done, she went back to the streets to see if there were any other people who needed assistance. All was quiet for the time being. Branyrd walked toward the park where she had convinced the previous robbers to unhand their goods. They had scattered and were nowhere in sight.

Next Branyrd walked the streets and began clearing up the glass that was all over the street from the windows that had been shattered when the robbers had broken into the stories. Some of the owners came out to see her.

"We were going to do that. You do not need to injure yourself, miss," one man replied as he carried a broom and a dustpan and began to clear out the glass.

"I am here to help. Please let me help you."

"Thank you. I saw what you did with those men who stole from my neighbor's store. That was brave of you to take them all on. Who are you?"

"I am Branyrd. That is my mission to help all of you here on Earth. HE has sent me in answer to all the prayers HE has received."

"Do you mean GOD has sent you here? Are you an Angel?"

"Yes, I am HIS messenger.

The man was stunned to silence over her words and turned back to his store to bring others out to see her.

When he came back, Branyrd had finished clearing out all the glass off the sidewalk and street in front of the store fronts. She turned to face the crowd that had gathered in front of her.

The people got down on their knees in front of the Angel and cried. "Our prayers were heard and answered. Thank you, GOD!"

"Please do not bow down to me. You only bow down to HIM."

The people quickly stood up at her words.

"Can you stop all this violence and keep us safe?" one man asked.

"I will do my best with your help."

"How can we help? We are unable to stop them from repeatedly stealing from us. We cannot live like this and take care of our families. We can't afford to keep losing our inventory in this way," the owner stated, upset and disheveled.

Another stated, "The police are no help here. They cannot control all this stealing and pillaging. The robbers come in packs and overpower not only us but also the police."

"Yes, I understand that. But you must be strong and keep praying to HIM. HE listens to you and will do all HE can to make your lives safe once again. That is why I am here."

"I am here also to help," Benedicto replied as he came up behind Branyrd and startled her.

"Where have you been, Guardian Angel?" Branyrd added with a frown.

"I have been right here with you, Angel, like always."

"Hmm, I see." Branyrd rolled her eyes at him causing him to chortle.

One owner spoke up in alarm when she spotted the huge man who appeared to come out of thin air. "Who are you?"

"I am Benedicto, here to aid Branyrd in any way I can in her mission."

"Mission? What do you mean?" the owner asked.

Branyrd replied, "This is my Mission of Hope to stop the violence and aid you in any way we can to get your city back and make these perpetrators pay for their evil deeds."

"I pray that you can do all that. We don't know what else to do on our own," another person stated.

"What do you want us to do now?" a man asked.

"I think you should clean up your stores inside and stay there until I can make sure no more problems are coming this way."

"That we can do," one man stated, and pushed the crowd back to their own stores.

Branyrd and Benedicto stood guard over the stores and walked back and forth to assure the people there that they were here to help.

Branyrd whispered to Benedicto, "It looks like there will not be any more problems tonight. We can't let our guard down though. I'm sure they are gathering to return soon."

"Yes, I believe they are. We need to replace the windows in the stores to keep anyone from entering again."

"Let's replace them with something stronger than glass to deter them from doing the same thing," Branyrd said.

"I agree. We can put up metal sheeting. That will keep them out. I know where I can get some," he announced as he flew away once again.

"I hope you come back soon," Branyrd whispered as she looked around for anything else she could do until he returned.

The original owner called out to Branyrd from his open store front," Can I get you some coffee or something to eat, Branyrd?"

"Thank you. I would love some coffee if it is not too much trouble. That is one thing I have grown accustomed to while I have been here."

"Do you need cream or sugar?"

"No, black will be fine. Thank you."

"Have you been to Earth before this?"

"Yes, I have. This is my fourth mission."

"You call this a mission. Why is that?"

"Well, the LORD listens to your prayers and gives HIS messengers missions or jobs, to complete in order to move up the levels of Angel status."

"Really? Is that how HE does it? I didn't realize that Angels have different status levels as such."

"Yes, we do. We need to prove that we can complete our jobs as they are given to us. If we do, we move up the ladder, so to speak."

"Where are you on the ladder, can I ask?"

"Of course. I am an Angel First Class now. But there are others who are higher than I am like Benedicto. He is a Guardian Angel First Class Most High. I may never attain that level."

"Oh, I see. I guess. It is all so surprising. I never met an Angel before. I only hope and pray that I will meet you again one day in Heaven, if HE thinks I am worthy."

"I am sure HE is already saving you a place there."

"Thank you so much. I will earn HIS trust and work hard to be better each day."

"I'm sure you will, sir. Don't worry about your windows, we will fix them. Benedicto is on his way back here with some metal sheeting to do just that. You can be assured that no one will get into your store after we do this."

"I don't know how to thank you both. My wife and fellow store owners will be happy to hear this. If you need anything else, please let us know. We live upstairs in the apartments above our stores. Feel free to come up if you need anything."

"No need to thank us. Please take care of your family and stay inside tonight. There could be more trouble coming."

"I'm sure there will be. They always come back for more."

The man bowed to Branyrd, took the empty coffee cup, and turned to go back to his family.

Branyrd waved her hands over the man's head as she heard him pray that he would be safe from harm along with his family.

CHAPTER EIGHTEEN

Benedicto returned with a truck load of sheeting and several men who were going to put it up.

"How did you convince these men to do this?"

"Well, I told them that we are the LORD'S messengers and that HE is requesting that they do this to pave their way to Heaven."

"They believed you?"

"Well, of course, they did. Once I melted one of the sheets of metal in front of their eyes, they promised to do whatever HE requested of them."

"Hmm, I see. I wonder if HE will approve of that?"

"Well, I did ask HIS permission first, Angel." Benedicto winked at her and gave the men instructions to begin the project.

There was plenty of noise as the men hammered the sheets into place on all the store fronts that would keep anyone from entering until they could replace them with glass again.

Meanwhile the police were being kept quite busy interrogating all the men that Benedicto had dropped off. They were soon aware of the noise outside that was caused by all the hammering.

The captain appointed several officers to investigate the racket that could be heard a few blocks away.

When the officers arrived, the men were almost finished putting up the sheets of metal. The workers stopped to talk with the officers and explain what they were doing.

One worker explained, "We are only doing our duty, officers. We want to go to Heaven and this is one way that we may be able to do that."

"What? What are you talking about?" the lead officer asked, puzzled at the man's response.

"See that large man over there with the beautiful woman?"

"Did they tell you to do this?"

"Yes, officer. Sorry, but we need to get back to the warehouse now."

"Okay, be on your way. I will find out more about this," the officer said as he headed over to see the large man and beautiful woman who appeared to wear a halo of gold around her head that encased her long flowing golden hair. He could not take his eyes off of her. He had never seen anyone like this before. She surely was not from this world, he thought.

Branyrd saw the police heading their way and smiled. As she smiled her halo grew brighter, almost blinding them as they got closer.

The officers were shaken from this brilliant light that emanated from behind the woman. They didn't know what to make of this since it was night time and there were no lights around her.

One officer who finally cleared his head and voice asked, "Who are you and why did you tell those men...what you told them to do?"

"What did they tell you, officer?" Branyrd asked as her smile grew in brilliance along with her halo.

"I...I don't know. I forgot." He shrugged his shoulders and looked at his fellow officers with a puzzled expression.

The officers looked at Branyrd one more time and then turned and walked away back to their precinct.

Benedicto laughed and said, "Well, I guess you told them, Angel. Didn't you?"

"There was nothing to say, Benedicto, as you well know." She smiled and winked at him before turning to inspect the metal sheeting that was now in place.

Several of the owners of the stores were already there looking it over and smiling.

"Thank you, Angels, for doing this. This should keep out any more offenders until we can afford to replace all the glass and get some metal gates to close over the windows at night."

"That is a good idea, gentleman," Branyrd said and shook hands with them all as they each came forward to thank her and Benedicto.

One owner made an observation about Benedicto. "I am not surprised that you convinced these men to install the sheeting. One look at you and I would do anything you requested of me."

The Guardian Angel nodded and smiled. "I think the men were good God-fearing men who only wanted to do what was right in HIS eyes."

"I guess you are right about that. But we thank you both again for what you have done for us. What can we do for you in return?"

"There is nothing you need to do but keep you and your families safe from harm and do the best you can do each day in HIS name. Things will get better, we assure you."

"We will do our best," one man responded as the others nodded in agreement.

"Can we offer you something to eat or drink or a place to stay?" one woman asked.

"Thank you, but the LORD will take care of us. We have much more work to do. Take care and pray if you need anything else."

"That we will do," several responded.

The people watched the Angels as they walked away and disappeared in a flash of light. They looked at each other in disbelief. They could not explain what they had witnessed.

CHAPTER NINETEEN

The LORD called out to the Angels to go to the park where they had been previously.

They flew there and landed a distance away from some men who were gathered near a bench where a woman sat.

Branyrd whispered, "What is going on here? Does she need our help?"

"It looks like they are just talking for now, Angel. But I think they have more in mind than talking."

"Let's go closer so we can see what they are talking about."

They heard the woman cry out as they got closer. "Please don't hurt me! I am not a threat to you. I have children in the tent who need me. I don't have anything of value. Please go away!"

Benedicto stepped forward and tapped the lead man on the shoulder who was leaning over the woman and threatening to harm her. The man turned around in shock to see this huge man looking down on him.

"Who…who are you? Where did you come from?" he asked with a shaky voice.

"I should be asking you that question and others."

"I wasn't going to hurt her. We are just leaving. No need to start a fight."

"I think that would be a good idea."

Branyrd watched from a distance as the men quickly dispersed, fearful of looking behind them in case the Guardian Angel was after them.

"Are you all right?" Branyrd asked the woman who looked shocked to see her and Benedicto standing in front of her while just a moment ago she was in danger of being possibly raped and murdered in front of her children.

"I…I…am okay. But where did you come from? I can't thank you enough. If you hadn't come by, I would be…."

"Do not worry about it now. No one is going to harm you or your children."

"Thank goodness they are sleeping and didn't hear any of this. They are too young to understand the problems of this world."

"We want to help you. What you need is a safe place for you and your children to sleep. Come with us. We will find a shelter for you all."

"I tried that already. The shelters were all full. There was no room for us. I had to set up my tent or what's left of it and get them some scraps to eat so that they could sleep."

"We will fix all that. Come with us."

The woman sighed heavily and woke her children to explain, "We are going to find a bed to sleep in."

"But, Mommy, you said there wasn't any place for us to sleep," the younger child retorted.

"I know, but these nice people said they would find a place for us. Now let's gather our stuff and go with them."

"Who are they, Mommy?" the oldest child asked.

"I don't know but I feel it in my heart that they are good people who have come to help us. Now hurry up and grab your teddy and blanket."

The children nodded half asleep and followed their mother to where the two people were waiting for them.

Branyrd bent down to greet the two young children, "Hi, there is no need to be afraid. We are here to help you and your mommy find a nice warm place to stay. Okay?"

"Okay," they responded as they became fascinated when they saw the light behind the lady's head.

They whispered to each other, "Do you see that? There is a light on her head. What is that?"

"I don't know but it could be a halo. I saw one like that on GOD in church and on several of the Angels. Maybe they are Angels?"

"Really? Are they really Angels?"

Benedicto listened to the children talking softly as he walked behind them. "Do you want me to carry you? You look very tired."

"You are a big man! How come you are so tall?" the older child asked in awe.

"Yes, I am quite large. I guess that is the way the LORD made me."

"GOD made you like that?" the younger child asked in surprise.

"Yes."

"Will we be that big when we get older?" the older child asked.

"Maybe or maybe a little smaller."

"Can you carry us? We are kind of tired."

"Hop up into my arms and I will lift you both up on my shoulders."

There were whoops and hollers of delight as the children settled on Benedicto's shoulders.

"What is your name, big man?" the older child queried.

"I am known as Benedicto. What are your names?"

The older boy answered for them, "I am Liam and my brother is Noah. I am six and Noah is four. How old are you, Benedicto?"

"Haha, I am older than time."

"Huh? I don't understand," Liam stated with a frown.

"That's very old, Liam."

"Oh, like our mother. She is old too!"

Their mother laughed when she heard their words. "I guess they consider me old. Some days I do feel it too. Life is hard on the streets. I don't know how long I can keep doing this and protect them from all the dangers around us, like those men."

"Yes, I understand," Branyrd patted the woman on her shoulder as they walked together.

"I'm sorry. I should introduce myself to you. I am Arianne."

"Hi Arianne. It's nice to meet you and your boys. I am Branyrd, sent here to help you. HE heard your prayers."

"I…don't understand. Do you mean GOD heard my prayers?"

"Yes, HE hears everyone's prayers. That is why HE sent us here to help you."

Arianne began to cry and couldn't move forward as she crumbled to the ground.

Branyrd pulled her up and held her as they continued to walk. "It will be all right. Don't worry. We are here to make sure that you and your sons are safe before we leave."

"I…I pray every night and never thought that HE had heard me or wanted to help me. I am not a good person. I have done things that I regret."

"HE knows everything about you and that you are sorry for your sins. HE forgives you."

"I...I can't believe this! How can this be? Are you an Angel?"

"Yes, we are HIS messengers and do HIS bidding. Now here is the place I mentioned. They have room for you. Come in."

Arianne and her sons followed the Angels into the large hall where many cots were empty and waiting for them. The children got all excited once they were helped down from Benedicto's shoulders and raced each other to claim a cot.

"I don't know how to thank you both."

"You are welcome. Now get your children settled. There is a cafeteria in the next room that has food waiting for you. There is everything you will need here. Stay here and get acclimated. You do not have to leave here ever but if you want to, you can. It would be best to stay to keep your children safe and well fed."

"What do I have to do? Will I need to pay them for all this?"

"No, but you can offer to help in the café, by making up new cots for others or in any other way that you are needed. The children will also need to be schooled. There is a school here run by the people who care for this facility."

"I can't understand any of this. It is all a miracle! I am not deserving." Arianne bent her head and shed more tears.

"No more crying, Arianne. Your life will be better now. Work hard here and you will be fine, all of you."

"Thank you again, Branyrd and Benedicto. I will never forget what you have done for us."

"No need to thank us, just stay safe here with your children. All things will work out for you. Keep praying and thanking

HIM, not us. For HE is the one who makes all things possible."

"I will." Arianne sniffled and wiped her tears on her sleeve.

"Mommy, can we get something to eat now? I can smell hot dogs. Those kids over there said there is a lot of food and they even have some extra clothes and toys to share with us."

"Yes, of course. Let's go." Arianne smiled at her boys' joy and turned to look for the Angels but they were gone. She looked up and whispered, "thank you."

CHAPTER TWENTY

Branyrd heard HIS voice in her head telling her to go to the police station now.

"We better hurry, Benedicto. There is a lot of trouble with those men you dropped off there. They are out of control."

"Let's go, Angel."

They stood outside the door of the police station and could hear all the noise inside. They opened the door and stepped inside.

The police were holding many of the men at gunpoint as they struggled to keep the men in check. They fastened handcuffs on many of them but others were still fighting to get away.

Benedicto stepped forward and asked, "Can I give you a hand, officer?"

One officer jumped back in alarm when he looked up at the large man who had just spoken to him.

"Who are you?"

Another officer came by and answered for Benedicto. "He is the one who brought all these men here earlier."

"Hmm, I see. I don't know why you did that or how. These men are uncontrollable. They are not afraid of us and will not settle down even when in cells or handcuffed."

"I will take care of that," Benedicto responded as he grabbed four men and held them together in both hands as they continued to kick out at him.

One man looked up at the Guardian Angel and called out to his fellow perpetrators, "This is the guy who brought us in here. Who does he think he is?"

"I am HIS messenger. That is who I am. I am known as Benedicto."

"What are you saying, big man? Who is HE?" another man asked, keeping a distance.

"I am here to help you. I don't want to hurt you but if you do not cooperate, I may have to."

"You better listen to him. I saw what he could do. He took out several men who were trying to shoot up the street. They are not here now," another man explained in handcuffs.

"Did he kill them?"

"I don't know. I didn't stick around to find out."

"Do any of you have another question to ask of me?" Benedicto stood tall and fierce and appeared to grow even larger in front of their eyes.

"No sir. We don't have any more questions." The man turned to the other men and said, "Listen guys, we better settle down or else. I don't trust this man."

One man was stupid enough to test Benedicto when he tried to push the Angel from behind. Benedicto turned and lifted the man up by his pants and hung him upside down, kicking and screaming.

"What did you have to say for yourself?" he asked the frightened man.

"Nothing, Nothing at all." The man called out to the police, "Please put me in a cell away from this man now!"

The officers began to chuckle as each man stood at attention and kept their eyes on Benedicto, afraid to move.

"Okay, let's get back to your cells. We aren't finished with you yet. We have a lot of questions for all of you and we want the truth," one officer instructed.

"That is right, gentlemen. Make sure you tell these good officers the truth or else I will be back," Benedicto said as he shook hands with the officers in charge and saluted them on his way out. "Keep up the good work, officers."

The officers saluted him back and smiled as they yelled out thanks to the large man.

Branyrd stood at the doorway and watched all this play out. She didn't have to say a thing. Benedicto had taken care of all of it. She smiled at the officers and followed her Guardian Angel out of the precinct.

"I guess you didn't need my help with any of that."

"Of course, I did. You had my back, did you not, Angel?"

"Yep, of course, I did!" Branyrd giggled as she looked at him with his quirky eyebrow thing going on again.

"Have you considered what our next step will be, Angel?"

"I'm not sure. I feel that there is more to do here that we are not seeing. Maybe HE will tell us where we are needed."

Branyrd smiled and began walking toward a business section of the town. She stopped in front of a newspaper office.

"Let's go inside here. I think we may be needed here."

"Lead the way, Angel. I have your back," he guffawed.

The office was in full swing as people hurried back and forth getting to one office or another, answering the many ringing telephones and pecking away at computers.

Branyrd stood looking at a man who was hunched over his computer and working the keys frantically.

"What are you writing about, sir?" she asked him.

He looked up in alarm not hearing her come up beside him. "Who are you?"

"Oh, I am just a visitor here. I was wondering what you are writing so furiously."

"It is my job to find interesting stories to put into the newspaper. There is violence on our streets. Haven't you noticed?"

"Yes, I certainly have. There is danger in the streets for innocent people."

"Yes, that too. There are so many deaths and drive-by shootings that I can't keep up with them."

"I see. Do you have any good stories to write about, such as the good that is happening around you?"

"What good? I don't see any good happening here. Everyone is out to get the other guy. It is a dog-eat-dog world. Don't you know that, lady? Who are you anyway? Why all the questions?"

"Well, I would like to share some good stories with you to put in your newspaper for the next edition."

"Are you kidding me? That doesn't sell. Only violence, murder, rape, kidnapping, stuff like that sells today."

"You really believe that?"

"Yes, I not only believe it, I see it with my own eyes."

"That's too bad. I had so many wonderful things to share with you. Well, I guess I will find someone else to share these stories with. Good day, sir."

Branyrd left his cubicle and went to another where a woman was staring at her screen and shaking her head.

"What's wrong, miss?"

"Who are you? Where did you come from?"

"Oh, I am just a visitor here and looking for someone to share some good-feeling stories. Are you interested in writing about something good for a change?"

"Maybe that is what I need to hear. I am so tired of all this violence, bloodshed, watching it on TV, in the media and in our newspaper. Our boss wants us to write about all this and won't listen to anything else."

"That is sad. Do you want to hear some stories that will lift your spirits?"

"Sure, I could use something positive. I feel the angst and troubles of the world and my shoulders are getting heavier each day."

"Let me lighten your load, Siarra."

"How…how do you know my name?"

"HE told me."

"Who?"

"HE did. HE knows everyone and everything."

"I don't understand. Who are you talking about? Wait a minute. Is this one of those TV shows where you have a hidden camera on me?" Siarra looked around for some evidence of this.

"No, I don't have a camera. HE doesn't need one."

"Please, I don't know who you are or what you want of me."

"I don't want anything of you, Siarra. I want to lighten your burdens. I can feel your pain and how working here has made you more depressed than ever."

"Yes, I do feel more depressed each day I spend working here. It is awful hearing all these horrendous things and having to write about them."

"Will you listen to me and let me help you? That is why I am here. I am Branyrd, the LORD's messenger."

"What? GOD sent you?"

"Yes, HE did. HE has felt your pain and wanted to relieve the stress you are under. Will you let me do that for HIM?"

"I don't know what to say?"

"Just say 'yes,' Siarra."

Siarra broke down and shed tears that she didn't know she was holding inside. She immediately felt lighter.

Branyrd stepped closer and embraced her, keeping her tightly in her arms and wrapping her wings that were invisible around the woman.

Siarra sighed in a good way and smiled as she snuggled closer to the Angel.

"I do feel much better. Thank you, Branyrd. I don't know what you did but I am grateful. I have been feeling a darkness coming over me and haven't been able to think of anything but evil things. It has been so exhausting."

"Yes, I understand. I felt the evil leaving you. It is now gone. What you must do from now on is write only about positive things for the paper."

"But…but my editor won't allow it. He will fire me!'

"I don't think he will. I will speak with him. Stay here and I will let you know what he says."

CHAPTER TWENTY-ONE

Siarra watched the beautiful lady walk into the editor's office and sit down. She observed the editor's facial expressions to try to interpret what was being said. She could tell that her boss was surprised but not angry as he usually is. She waited patiently at her desk for Branyrd to return.

Siarra studied their expressions as Branyrd shook the editor's hand, left his office and headed back to her cubicle.

"What did he say, Branyrd? I can't wait to hear. He didn't look upset or angry. That is a good sign."

"Yes, he was quite pleasant after I introduced myself and explained why I was here."

"Did he understand what you were saying about GOD?"

"I think he is a good man, just overworked and under pressure to sell his papers. I don't think he realized how all this negative news was affecting his staff. He apologized and promised to write more positive news from now on. He even suggested that you have a new column for that kind of news – happy and uplifting stories."

"Really? He said that I can write about good things for a change?"

"Most definitely. Let me give you a few to start you off. Okay?"

"By all means, I need all I can get to begin this new adventure. I can't thank you enough, Branyrd."

"Just try to stay positive and don't let all the negativity get you down again. If you feel that it is infringing on your energy again just pray to HIM. HE listens to everyone's prayers and will send you strength and courage to continue to do what is right."

"I will do that, Branyrd. Now please share some of these stories with me so I can begin this new column."

Branyrd pulled up a chair and shared what had been happening since she and Benedicto had arrived there, how people were being taken care of and how they were kept safe from harm.

Siarra typed her notes as she listened with tears streaming. She stopped every so often to blow her nose and wipe her tears. She kept a smile on her face the entire time as she nodded and kept typing.

Benedicto came up behind Branyrd and tapped her on the shoulder. Did you find what you needed to do here, Angel?"

"Yes, most definitely, I did. Right, Siarra?"

Siarra couldn't answer her right away because she was in awe over this large man who now stood in front of her.

"Oh, please let me introduce you to my Guardian Angel, Benedicto. He is here to help me spread the LORD's word."

"I…I…don't know what to say. It's an honor to meet both of you. I've never seen anyone like you, Benedicto! I apologize for staring."

"That's quite all right. I do frighten some people. I hope you are not frightened of me. I am not here to harm you, only to help you and others. It's a pleasure to meet you too, Siarra."

"I'm happy to hear that. I would love to have a Guardian Angel like you to keep all the evil away."

"That is my job, Siarra. That is what I do, fight against evil. I will keep an eye on you too."

"Thank you so much. I need all the help I can get. I feel blessed to have both of you here to pave the way for me. I was lost and thought that I would die from unhappiness."

"No worries about that. Keep positive and spread this positivity around. It is contagious."

"I will do my best. Thank you both. Thank you also, Branyrd, for these amazing stories. I can't wait to begin my first column. I hope that I can spread good over evil and lighten the loads of readers everywhere."

"I think you will do that quite well, Siarra," Branyrd said as she patted her on the back and left the room with Benedicto.

The Angels looked back at Siarra as the woman now sat up straighter while her face glowed with happiness.

"It looks like you had another successful addition to your mission, Angel."

"Thank you, Benedicto. I do feel lighter myself seeing Siarra happy and less stressed. Her aura was getting quite dark. Did you notice?"

"Yes, I did notice that, Angel. But I knew that you would succeed. You always do." Benedicto winked at Branyrd and stood listening as HIS voice filled their heads once again.

CHAPTER TWENTY-TWO

Branyrd listened to HIM as HE explained what she needed to tackle next.

"Can we do this, LORD? He is the most important leader in this country. How can we change history?"

"You don't have to change history. All you must do is give him courage to do what is right by leading MY people in the right direction."

"I see. We will do our best."

"There is too much corruption in the world. It has to stop. I don't want to end it all. They must find a way to get back on track and do what is right for everyone without any harm coming to anyone. That is all I ask."

"Where do we go now, LORD?"

Branyrd didn't have to wait for long, because she and Benedicto were flown to a large white building. They stood outside and waited for further instructions, but none came. They proceeded to walk to the front door.

Several men came from all directions with guns pointed at them.

Benedicto stepped forward and raised his hands causing the men to lower their guns and drop them at their sides.

"We are not here to harm anyone. We have been sent by HIM to help you."

"Who is HIM?" one man asked in confusion over how he had lost control of his gun and now couldn't move an inch from where he stood.

"HE is the LORD. HE has sent us here to stop wars from happening all over the world.

Branyrd spoke up in a soft and soothing voice to calm the startled men and women who stood there befuddled, "I am Branyrd and this is Benedicto. We are not here to cause any harm as he already told you. We only need to speak with your leader."

"We cannot do that. We are not allowed to give anyone entrance. We do not know you or believe what you claim."

"We understand that you have a job to do. But our job is to speak with this man and prevent wars from destroying your world and many innocent people."

Benedicto raised his hands again along with Branyrd and instructed the men to lead the way for them to their leader.

The men and women formed a line and escorted the Angels into the main office of their leader who looked up in alarm.

"Who are these people? Why did you allow them entrance without announcing them?" The man's voice raised in anger as he studied each of his guards for someone to explain.

"Sorry to bother you, Mr. President, but we are here on our own mission as messengers of the LORD," Branyrd explained since the men and women were unable to speak.

"Who are you? Do you think I am naïve enough to believe something so preposterous as this. Who are you really?"

"We are who we said we are, sir. I am Benedicto and this is Branyrd. We are messengers of the LORD sent here to assist you in preventing a world war. The LORD has instructed us to help you make decisions that will be safe for all. HE does not want to see the world end this way. There are many innocents here. You must make the right decision now to prevent wars from beginning all over the world. You have the power to do this."

"I do not understand any of this. How can this be? HE sent you here to help me? I prayed for help but didn't realize that HE heard me. What can I do to prevent this war? I know I have to do something. I don't want the world to end."

Branyrd came closer and raised her hands over the man to calm him. "I am going to come closer and sit down so we can talk about this. Please do not be alarmed. You are not in danger in any way. None of you are in danger. Please listen to me. I am here to help you and others on Earth. There are many evil factions that are in power now and pushing their way to the top to prevent others from doing good. We are here to stop the evil that is growing."

"I can feel it too. I am trying to do what is right but there are others who are working against me. How can I do this without causing any harm to my people and others?"

Branyrd continued, "We will help you. We plan to visit others in power to persuade them to do the right thing too, but you must be the first to do that. The rest of the world will follow in the same manner."

The leader held his head in his hands and sighed. "I feel overwhelmed by all of this and especially your appearance. I can't believe this is happening. I always believed in HIM but never imagined that HE would send you to help me. Are you Angels?"

"Yes, we are HIS messengers of peace and hope. What you must do is set up a conference with all leaders of the world and carry on a dialogue through all this. Let them know that war is not the answer."

Benedicto stood by and let Branyrd take charge of this meeting. He smiled and calmed the men around him who wanted to move closer. He would not allow them to do that just yet.

The leader nodded to the Angels, called his staff together and arranged for a conference call with all the leaders. It would take a little time to complete but he would do all he could to accomplish this since he knew that HE was on his side and helping him.

Branyrd smiled at the leader and said, "We will leave you to do this now. We have others to help. Be strong and resilient in your role and always know that HE is near if you need HIM."

"Thank you both. Now I have much work to do."

Branyrd and Benedicto disappeared in front of the puzzled men and women who were still standing guard in the room but now were able to move around. They searched for the two people who were there a minute ago but without any sign of where they went. They picked up their weapons and continued their search around the building and outside to no avail. All they could do now was shake their heads as they locked eyes with one another in disbelief.

The Angels were next directed to another part of the world where trouble was paramount to many innocents. The Angels were sent into tunnels and buildings in search of people who were being held hostage. They pulled others out of cells and collected them all in their arms. There were too many to count but the Angels held them firmly under their wings as they flew them to safety.

Bullets soared past them as the kidnappers continued to barrage them with bullets to prevent them from taking the hostages away. The Angels kept the bullets away from the people who cried out in fear not knowing what was happening. The Angels explained in a calm manner that they were being flown to a hospital for care and later would be transported to their homelands.

Once the Angels safely landed at a hospital, they guided the people to nurses who were on duty and thoroughly confused to see all these people suddenly appear in their emergency room.

Branyrd explained, "Sorry to inundate you with all these patients but I think you may want to alert the authorities about them. They are the hostages that were taken by warring factions against other nations. They have been held hostage for many months and are in dire need of medical care."

"But…how.?"

Benedicto stepped forward and continued, "Don't worry about how this was done, please take care of them and contact the police to let them know that these people are now here. I am sure the families will want to know that they are now safe."

"I…I…just a minute." The nurse rushed to the phones after getting others to take care of the bedraggled people who were sitting all over the room for treatment.

She told the police what the large man had conveyed to her. She kept looking at the huge man and beautiful lady who were standing next to her expecting them to disappear or be a mirage.

The police responded that they would relate the message to the chief and he, in turn, would handle the situation. Officers were on their way there to take information from the two who brought them in and from the hostages themselves.

Word quickly spread throughout the hospital that the hostages were back. Some of them could not speak English and translators were enlisted to aid in treating them.

Before long news vans were lined up outside the hospital to get the latest scoop on this unbelievable rescue. They wanted to know who the rescuers were and how they had accomplished what others in many nations had been unable to do.

Branyrd and Benedicto stepped outside to meet the press and relate their story.

"We are Branyrd and Benedicto, messengers of the LORD. We were sent here to aid those in need all over the world."

"Who did you say sent you?" a reporter queried in a mocking tone.

"The LORD sent us. HE watches over everyone and everything. HE knows what has been happening to the world and how violence and evil has taken over," Branyrd explained.

"Are you saying that you are Angels sent from Heaven?" one reporter asked in disbelief.

"But how did you accomplish this feat when others have not been successful?" another press person asked.

"We did not do anything. It was all done by HIM. There is nothing HE cannot do. We are only HIS messengers of hope," Benedicto added.

"Well, now I have heard everything!" one reporter exclaimed as he shook his head and mumbled to himself.

"Why are you just coming now? There have been so many deaths, violence on our streets, people of all ages dying, women being raped, people being tortured and kidnapped like these people. Why did you not come sooner?" another asked in dismay.

"We are only HIS messengers. If you need to ask HIM this question you must pray to HIM and HE will answer you," Branyrd stressed.

"What if I don't believe in GOD? Will HE still listen to me?"

"Yes, HE listens to all who pray."

The man looked unsure what to do but turned and walked away with his head down.

Others stepped forward and asked more questions. "What made you come now? What happened that was different to spurn HIS attention toward the world now?"

"We do HIS bidding. Many have been praying for HIS intercession. That is why we are here now," Branyrd answered.

"We are lost and can't do this on our own. Will HE help us?" another reporter asked with tears in her eyes.

"Yes, HE will. That is why we are here. The more you pray the more HE will send down messengers to aid you."

There was a murmuring as more and more questions circulated. But soon they halted when several black vehicles pulled up outside the hospital entrance and many men and women alighted and headed inside.

CHAPTER TWENTY-THREE

The dark suited men and women spread around the hospital questioning everyone about what had just transpired. The nurse who had called the police stepped forward to explain, "I was the one who spoke with the two rescuers who brought these people here. They said these people were the hostages that many nations were waiting for but could not save."

"Where are these two people now?" the man in charge asked.

"Who are you people? Are you the police?" the nurse asked in confusion.

"No, we are from the government."

"Oh, I didn't call you. How did you...?" the nurse stuttered in disbelief.

"No concern of yours right now. We need to speak with the two rescuers. Where are they?"

The nurse looked around but didn't see them. "Maybe they left. I have been too busy to keep an eye on them. As you can see, we have been inundated since these hostages came here."

"We will find them. No problem." The man abruptly turned away and surveyed the room. He sent others outside to look further.

Branyrd and Benedicto watched as the men and women circulated around the hospital corridors looking in vain for them. The Angels had flown away after HE had summoned them. The reporters were too distracted by the arrival of the official-looking people to notice their absence.

Newspapers were soon reporting the miraculous rescue of the hostages from many nations by two mysterious rescuers who had disappeared. No one could answer the important question, "Who were these rescuers and how did they undertake this incredible mission?"

***

With all this happening, Siarra got her first immense, feel-good story to report. She raised her eyes up and whispered, 'Thank you, GOD.'

During this time each nation had met recently during a conference call to discuss the current situation of the escalation of possible wars around the world. The leaders soon received word of the hostages' return which took them away from their present problems.

Word spread far and wide as many nations contacted each other to find out who the rescuers were so that they could thank them, to no avail. They each actively worked to get their own people returned safely to their countries after they were treated.

***

The LORD watched what was transpiring as HE kept in contact with the Angels. "You have more to do, Angels. Your mission is not yet completed. Commendable job so far."

"Thank you, LORD. What do YOU need us to do next?" Branyrd asked as she smiled at Benedicto.

"There are some others who need rescuing from their lands that have been destroyed by other countries. I need you to go to these countries and help the people rebuild their homes and keep the warring factions away while you do this." HE opened a window so that the Angels could see their destinations.

"Yes, LORD. We will do our best." Branyrd exchanged puzzled looks with Benedicto who shrugged his shoulders and lifted her up to fly away to the designated areas that the LORD had shown them.

When they arrived, the land was totally destroyed. Everywhere they looked all they saw were metal structures, part of buildings that once stood there. The Angels began to look for the people. They were nowhere in sight.

They flew above the land and noticed some areas where some derelict buildings partially stood. They dropped down to inspect them.

Many women and children were inside and shocked to see these two people enter, especially the extremely large man and the beautiful lady with the golden hair. They pushed back into the shadows, amid the rubble, not knowing what to expect from these strangers who clearly did not look like they belonged there.

"Please do not be frightened," Branyrd and Benedicto spoke in their languages and waved their hands over the startled people who quickly calmed down.

"We are messengers of HIM. We have come to help you rebuild your homes and your country."

One old man stepped forward and spoke for the group, "Do you not know of the dangers out there? Who are you and where did you come from?"

"We have come from far above here only to help you. We are the LORD'S messengers. We know of the dangers and will do all we can to protect you so that you can rebuild your homes," Branyrd explained.

A woman holding her two children close cried out, "HE has sent you? HE has answered our prayers. Praise be to GOD."

A man asked, still confused, "What can we do? How can we rebuild? All the young men have gone to fight the war. There are only old men like me and women and children. We are not strong enough to rebuild."

"That may be so, but we can help you. We will find a place to begin. Stay here and we will be back shortly," Branyrd answered as she turned and walked out of the building.

The Angels walked further away and flew up into the sky to survey the land once again. They could see some tanks heading this way with many soldiers walking alongside, rifles hanging over their shoulders.

They flew down in front of the alarmed men who jumped back and stared as they raised their guns in front of them.

"No need to do that," Benedicto said as he stepped closer to the startled men and pulled their guns out of their hands with a wave of his own hands.

"What? How did you do that? Who are you?"

Branyrd spoke up as she stood next to Benedicto, "We are HIS messengers. You will leave this place and not return. These people have suffered enough. They need to rebuild their homes now. This war is over. No good will come out of more killing."

"But...but... we have orders to clear this place and take hostages back to our base. We cannot return without them."

"Who told you that?" Benedicto asked as he showed his most intimidating face.

"Our premier, must be obeyed or he will kill our families while we watch, then us," a terrified young soldier exclaimed as he fell at their feet.

"Nothing will happen to your family. Return home and we will make sure that you are all safe."

Benedicto followed the men as they trudged out of the devastated landscape.

"I will be back shortly, Branyrd. You can begin the transformation for the people now. The way is clear."

Branyrd went back to the people and instructed them to follow her. "I know a place where you can begin the cleanup of your land."

The old man called everyone together and said, "We need to listen to this woman. I don't know why I feel that way but there is something about her that makes me feel safe for the first time since this horrible war began. She was sent here from whomever and wherever to help us."

The old men, women and children followed the beautiful woman with the golden hair as they whispered to themselves that she was surely someone special and not from this world.

They were in awe of the bright light that was coming off of her head. It was lighting the way for them to follow her.

CHAPTER TWENTY-FOUR

Branyrd instructed the old men to search for whatever they could find among the rubble to build a shelter. The women and children helped do their share of the searching and brought back what they could to the woman with the golden hair.

While the people were busy doing this, Branyrd gathered supplies on her own and placed them in a large plot that she had cleared of debris so that the rebuilding could begin.

When the people came back with pieces of boards, bricks, stones and other broken pieces of their homeland, they were amazed at what they saw.

Branyrd smiled at them and thanked them for their hard work. She explained, "This is where you will begin your new homes. It may not be where you had your original homes before but this is a start for you to find shelter and begin anew."

"How will we know if we are safe? The soldiers will be back and bomb all that we rebuilt! They have continued to do this for months now. They keep moving us away," one distraught woman said.

"Yes, I can see that. The soldiers will not return. Benedicto is making sure of that. You are safe now. Let's begin to construct your new homes."

The men and women along with the children followed the golden lady's instructions as she continued to provide them with more supplies. They never stopped working but wondered in whispers to each other where this beautiful woman was obtaining these building supplies.

Branyrd raised her hands over the construction to help it along. She brought in food and water for the hungry, thirsty and tired workers who did not question how she did this either. They were grateful for whatever they could have.

She instructed the workers to rest inside the building that was now all framed. While they rested, she finished the building with the LORD's help and left to find Benedicto.

Benedicto was inside the president's meeting room along with the soldiers he had brought there. The president or premier was not at all pleased to see this man and wanted explanations as he focused angry looks toward all his men who were refusing to meet his eyes.

"Who are you? Who do you think you are to come here and tell me what to do about my lands?"

"I come here with HIS instructions. I do not do anything without HIS word."

"Who are you speaking of?" The premier grew angrier with each word the large man uttered.

"I am here as HIS messenger," Benedicto repeated, calmly.

"If you do not tell me who you are talking about, I will be forced to kill you. Do you understand what I am saying?"

"Yes, I do but you do not understand what I am telling you."

The premier waved to his guards to take this man away. The guards shook their heads and backed away.

"Did you hear what I said? Take this imbecile away now!"

The men moved toward the huge man but could not get any closer. There appeared to be a wall keeping them from getting near him. They shook their heads and pushed with their hands in front of them but could not move.

"What is wrong with all of you? Get him and take him away now!"

"Sorry, Premier, but we cannot get any closer. There seems to be a wall all around him. We cannot break it down."

The premier moved toward the man and found that he was stuck in place a few feet away and also unable to move any closer.

"What have you done to me?" the premier exclaimed in alarm. "Stop this right now! I command you!"

"Sorry I do not take orders from anyone but the LORD!"

"Who is this LORD you speak of?"

"HE is the LORD of all of us. I only do HIS bidding. HE sent me here to stop this war and that is what I am going to do."

"You cannot do this. I am the ruler here in this land and soon to be in others. No one can stop me!"

"Only one can do this. HE is the one who can do all things."

"Let me go now!"

"I will if you promise to cease and desist from destroying any more people and lands. If you do not, HE will destroy you and all you hold dear."

The premier dropped to the ground in surrender. He did not know what to do. His men did the same and fell to their knees begging the intimidating man to release them.

Benedicto raised his hands over them and let them move away as Branyrd flew down and stood beside him.

"Who are you? How did you get here?" The premier asked in confusion as he looked at the woman who appeared to be wearing a golden halo too bright to look at for long.

"I am Branyrd, HIS messenger as is Benedicto here."

"I don't understand any of this. I want you to leave now and never return."

"We plan on doing that but you must promise first to stop this war, killing innocents and taking what is not yours."

"If I do, will you leave me alone?"

"Yes, but we will be watching you and making sure that you keep your promise to bring peace to these peoples and help them restore their land."

Men all around them dropped their guns and walked away and headed back to the people, who a short time ago, they were going to capture.

Branyrd watched the men and followed behind them to make sure they had good intentions toward the people she had just left.

Benedicto raised his hands over the premier to ensure that the man remembered the warning and would not harm anyone else.

When Benedicto arrived back to the people and the Angel, he saw that Branyrd was helping the men build some more houses for the displaced people. He came alongside her and whispered, "Looks like you got things under control here, Angel."

"I hope so, Benedicto. I wasn't too sure about these men when they headed back here. I followed to make sure they were not here to harm anyone. It looks like they decided to help these poor people instead."

***

The premier was still shaking his head over what had transpired. He called out to more of his men to return and take the lives of both of those strangers along with the men who had deserted him.

"You will take no prisoners. Do you understand me? No prisoners," he proclaimed as his face grew flushed and angry.

His men stood still but shook their heads at their leader. They were afraid to move one way or the other.

"Why are you still here? Did you not understand what I said? I will be forced to kill you all if you refuse to obey me!"

The men still did not move. They watched warily as their leader came closer to them. He now held a gun in his hand and put it against the first man's head.

"I will kill every one of you if you do not do as I say!" He pulled the trigger but the gun did not fire. He shook it and banged it against the ground as the shot rang out and a bullet entered his foot. He cried out in alarm and fell over.

The men watched their leader in agony but did not go to help him. Instead, they turned away and went to find their fellow soldiers who had left previously. It was as if someone or something was calling them there.

CHAPTER TWENTY-FIVE

The Angels were assisting the soldiers and the people to build their homes faster now with all the extra help that kept coming their way. More and more soldiers were arriving now as the Angels stepped aside to allow them to finish up the buildings.

Benedicto laid out some more wood for the homes and added some bricks for their chimneys. The men picked up the new materials without thinking about where they were coming from and continued at a feverish pace to complete each building.

Soon others were arriving with more supplies, furniture, food and materials to aid in the project causing the Angels to smile and raise their hands up to the LORD in thanks.

"Well, it looks like they have things under control now, Angel. We should move along to see what we can do for others in need."

"Did HE tell you this, Benedicto? I didn't hear HIM."

"Well, not exactly but soon you will receive word to assist others."

"I know there are many others in need but how can we be everywhere at once?"

"HE will make sure that we are. There is nothing for you to worry about, Angel."

Before they could continue their conversation, HE spoke, "Here is a window for you to see where you should travel next. There are still many others who are in need of your help."

The window opened and the Angels watched as men were being let out of jails and running wild in the streets. They were stealing cars, ransacking stores and killing people who tried to stop them.

"Where is this happening, LORD.," Branyrd asked in alarm.

"It is happening all over the world right now. You will go to each and every place. I will guide you there to stop this and warn the people if they don't desist that they will pay."

HE flew them to one of the jails and let them handle the situation as HE watched over them to provide protection from harm for them.

Benedicto stopped in front of the jail and pulled the men who were coming out aside. He picked them up and threw them back into their cells much to their shock. He kept going back out and picking up more men who were scurrying away to wreak havoc and bring them back to cells as the guards locked the men back in and looked up at the huge man in awe.

One guard asked, "Who are you? Where did you come from? Why are you doing this?"

"I was sent here by HIM. I am HIS messenger. Keep these men contained and do not let them out again."

The guards nodded and did as they were told, fearful that if they did not the giant of a man would harm them. They had never seen anyone like him, his size or his strength.

In the meantime, Branyrd was stopping the men who were in the stores from taking anything. She raised her hands over them and they had to drop everything that they had taken in their arms. They turned around to see what was preventing them from moving.

"Who are you? How did you do that?" were some of their questions as they stood transfixed in place by some unknown entity.

Other police were all over the street trying to herd the men back to the jail and noticed the giant moving through the crowds and picking up the escapees and carrying them in his arms back to the jail. They hurried over to the man to see who he was.

One officer tapped Benedicto on the shoulder, reaching up to do this, causing the Angel to turn around with several men in his grip.

The office asked, "How are you doing this and why? Who sent you here to help us? Was it the commissioner?"

"No, HE sent me to help you to get things under control."

"Who?"

"HE sent me. HE has seen the problems you are having and knows that you need support."

"Well, um...we appreciate all the support we can get but who sent you?" the officer probed further.

"The LORD. We are HIS messengers."

"We? Are there more of you?"

Branyrd stepped up behind the officer and announced, "Yes, I am HIS messenger also."

The officer turned around in alarm and was speechless when he saw this golden lady who glowed from behind even though there were no lights there to do that.

"I...don't understand." He rubbed his eyes and looked at her again to see if he was imagining all this.

"Please don't be alarmed. We do not want to harm anyone. We are only here at HIS directions to help you in any way we can."

"I see...I think. You are speaking of GOD. Is that who you are talking about?"

"Yes. HE is concerned about what is happening here on Earth. Things have gotten out of control and there is too much evil spreading everywhere."

"What are we supposed to do about it? We cannot contain it. There is too much for us to do without the necessary men. We have lost many men who have been killed trying to protect our cities and towns. How are we to do this?" the officer asked as he sighed heavily.

Branyrd placed her hand on his shoulder to calm the officer and responded, "We are here now and will do all we can to assist you in getting this place cleaned up. First, we must stop these men from running wild and return them to the jail where they will wait until they are tried for their crimes."

"Yes, I agree. That is what we have been trying to do. The giant over there is doing a commendable job of this right now. We could use several more of him. Will GOD send more down here to help us?"

"Not right now. We are the ones HE sent to do that."

"Please be careful, miss. You could get hurt. These men are dangerous and do not care if you are a woman or not. They will kill you if you get in their way."

"I can handle myself, officer, I assure you. I have HIS help at all times. I do not do anything without HIM."

"Oh, I see…I guess." The office watched as the golden lady pulled the men out of the store and directed them to go back to jail where they belonged. The men nodded in a stupor and did what Branyrd told them.

"I would never have believed this if I hadn't seen it with my own eyes," the officer said as he watched until the men went into the jail and were escorted by the shocked police who were waiting for them.

The store clerks rushed forward to thank the lady and began putting all the scattered merchandise back on the disheveled shelves.

A few officers followed the golden lady around to ensure that she was not harmed even after seeing what she was capable of doing in front of them. The men who she spoke to quickly did as she told them and rushed back to the jail without question.

The police quickly assisted the injured people who had been accosted by the escapees and sent them to the hospital in waiting ambulances after the golden lady had looked them over.

The police were in awe and kept blessing themselves and looking upward to say 'thanks.'

The Angels looked around to see if there were any stragglers who they had missed. They assisted the police in clearing out the streets of people who were walking around in a daze over what had transpired.

After one last look around, the Angels explained to the police that all should be peaceful. "If you need any more assistance, just pray to HIM. HE is always listening and answers all prayers."

"I...I will do that. I don't know how to thank you," the officer exclaimed as he shook their hands. He watched them walk away then disappear from sight.

The officer returned to the jail and would continually try to figure out what just happened and how. There would be much to discuss amongst themselves in the jail tonight. All he knew was that he would have to do more praying from now on.

CHAPTER TWENTY-SIX

The Angels flew over the area and watched as it was now quiet and calm. They waited to be guided to their next destination by HIS hand.

They traveled to another part of the world and watched some people as they went into a dilapidated house. They could hear screaming and fighting going on. It was time to investigate.

Branyrd and Benedicto flew in through a window in the back and approached two men who were fighting. They came between the startled duo who stopped with their fists in the air.

"What? Who are you?"

Branyrd let Benedicto take care of these two rowdy men who were smelling strongly of intoxication while she went into each room to see what else was going on and who had been screaming.

One room contained all women who were in different stages of dress. Others were drunk or on drugs and completely unconscious as she leaned over to check them.

One woman was crying in the corner with bedraggled clothes and knotted hair, her makeup was running down her face as her tears kept flowing.

"What happened to you? Are you all right?" Branyrd asked.

"Who are you? Are you a new girl to add to this mess? Turn around now and run away as fast and as far as you can."

Branyrd sat next to the distressed woman and laid her hand on her shoulder to calm her. "I am here to help you. We heard your cries and HE heard your prayers."

"Who is HE?"

"HE is the LORD of all of us. HE sent us here to help you and others find hope."

"What can you do to help us? You cannot take on all of these men. There are too many and they have weapons."

"Yes, I noticed that. Are you able to walk out of here?"

"How can I do that? There are men guarding both entrances. They won't let us go."

"Do as I say and you will not be harmed by any of them." Branyrd smiled at the woman and began to rouse the other women from their stupors to follow her out of this place.

The distraught woman did as the kind woman instructed and supported some of the other women out of the house. When they moved through the main room, they noticed that all the men were sitting around and not even looking at them. They hurried on their way and never looked back. When they got outside there was a police officer waiting for them and an ambulance.

Benedicto had made sure to keep the men under control. It hadn't taken much effort on his part. All he had done was pull the guns of their hands and bend them in half after the men tried to shoot him multiple times without harm.

They had been too shocked to move after that. He had told them to sit down until the police could get there. The dazed men nodded in agreement after what the giant had just done to their guns and to the other men who had been fighting and now lay unconscious on the floor.

Benedicto had alerted the authorities anonymously about the problems and the need for medical care at this house. All the women were taken away in the ambulance while the police went inside the building to find the men sitting around looking like they had seen a ghost. There were drugs, guns and other illegal items. Arrests were soon made and the men were escorted to jail.

The Angels left quickly through the same window in the back where they had previously entered. They looked up and heard HIS call once again to go to the next place.

They stood on a bridge that overlooked a stream of water. Along the banks of the water were many tents and people huddled together over a barrel with flames rising out of it.

"What do we have here, LORD?" Branyrd asked.

"Go see for yourself, Angel. These people need your help also."

Branyrd flew down and stopped in front of a young child who was playing in the water. "What are you doing, little boy?"

"Hi, do you want to see me float my boat?" the boy exclaimed as he waited for the beautiful golden lady to answer him.

"I would love to see you do that. I have never floated a boat before. Can you teach me how to do that?"

"Sure. I have some more bags to make into boats."

The Angel took a bag and followed instructions that the little boy gave her to create a boat.

"Yes! You did it right! Now we can both float boats together."

Branyrd smiled when she saw the joy in the boy's face as his boat floated away. He chased after it and brought it back to her.

"Now you can float yours, lady."

"Okay, here goes." Branyrd giggled as she saw that her boat floated a little before flipping over.

"Don't worry. You can make another one. That happens sometimes," the little boy announced with a serious expression.

"What is your name?"

"I am Ricardo. What is your name?"

"I am Branyrd. I am here to help you and all the others that are here."

"Why? We don't need help."

"Where are your parents, Ricardo?"

"I don't know. They left a while ago to get something for me to eat. I'm okay and not too hungry yet. Well, maybe a little."

"When was the last time you ate?"

"I don't remember. Maybe a few days ago," Ricard sighed.

"I will get you something to eat right away. Come with me."

Branyrd took Ricardo's hand and went to the other people who were inside tents and others sitting around.

"Do any of you have something for this boy to eat?"

People looked up at the golden lady and shook their heads. They went back to sleep or whatever they were doing and ignored her.

"Are any of you hungry?" Branyrd asked as she waited for some response.

"Yes, I am!" one disheveled man announced in clothes that hung on his emaciated body. A cigarette hung from his dry lips as he bent over and coughed.

"Me too!" an old woman stated as she pushed her way out of her holey tent to see who was speaking.

"Come with me if you want to eat."

The group suddenly came to life when they heard this and followed behind the golden lady and little boy.

Ricardo looked up at Branyrd and asked, "Where did you come from? I never saw you here before. You have golden hair and a light on your head."

"Yes, that is the halo that the LORD gave me."

"Will the LORD give me one too?" he asked.

"You have to ask HIM."

"Where is HE so that I can do that?"

"HE is everywhere, Ricardo, especially right here." Branyrd pointed to the boy's heart.

"But how can I see HIM?"

"You don't have to see HIM. HE sees you and hears everything you say."

"Can HE hear me now?"

"Yes, HE is listening."

"Okay, then I will ask HIM for a halo like yours."

Branyrd smiled and said, "HE said that one day you will have one."

"But how did you hear HIM say that? I didn't hear anything."

"That is because HE talks to me through my mind."

"Will HE talk to me through my mind too?"

"Maybe one day. Pray each day and you will hear HIM."

"I will? Can I pray now?"

"You can pray anytime you want. HE will always listen to you."

"Okay. I better tell my parents to do that too. They are always saying that no one listens to them. HE will listen, right?"

"Yes, HE will. Now let's go get you cleaned up and then you can eat your fill with everyone else."

Branyrd led the people to a washroom next to a store and restaurant where they could wash their hands and faces.

When they all filed out, she escorted them to a diner and told them that she could get them something to eat, whatever they wanted. Some yelled out that they wanted burgers, fries and milkshakes, others said eggs and steak, and still others wanted whatever she could get them.

The waitress shook her head after her manager saw all these homeless people sitting at several tables.

CHAPTER TWENTY-SEVEN

Benedicto came into the diner and spoke with the manager who nodded and shrugged his shoulders before giving his waitress the okay to take the orders.

Branyrd smiled at Benedicto and sat down at a table nearby with the little boy as he ate his fill of hotdogs, chips and pickles and a chocolate milkshake.

"Aren't you gonna have something to eat, Branyrd?"

"No, I'm not hungry. But maybe we can both have an ice cream after you are finished."

"Yay! I love ice cream. What kind do you like? I love strawberry ice cream!"

"Hmm, that is good too. I like dark chocolate ice cream and dark chocolate candy."

"I like all kinds of candy but I haven't had any for a long time though," the boy said, sadly.

"Well, I will get you some to bring back with you. Okay?"

"Oh yes! I would love that! What about my parents? Can I bring them something to eat too?"

"Of course. I will stay with you until they return."

"Can I go with you, Branyrd when you leave? I don't want to stay here anymore. My parents might not come back."

"Why don't you think they will come back, Ricardo?"

"I don't know. They have been gone a long, long time. I think something happened to them."

Branyrd exchanged looks with Benedicto who raised his quirky brow at her. She spoke to HIM in a prayer, "Please find Ricardo's parents."

HE replied, "I have already done that. They are not going to return. They are with ME now. They died from drug poisoning."

"What will happen to Ricardo now?"

"That is up to you, Angel. You must find someone to take care of him. That is part of your mission."

"I see. I will do my best, LORD."

Benedicto visited the manager to settle the bills for the people who filed out to return to their tents under the bridge. He waved his hand over the kitchen and left it spotless along with plenty of supplies, more than enough to make up for what the people had just eaten.

The manager looked up in amazement at the giant man and stuttered, "How did you do that? I don't understand."

"You do not have to understand. You have been kind to these people in letting them eat here. HE has rewarded you. You can thank HIM, not me." Benedicto turned and walked out of the restaurant to follow Branyrd and the others.

When the homeless people arrived at their tents, they found them all gone and everything was cleared away. They began yelling at the Angels to explain what happened.

"Where are our things? Where are we going to sleep now?"

Branyrd calmed them down and told them to follow her.

The people whispered to one another in confusion. "Where are we going? Who is she to do this?"

"We shouldn't complain. She got food for us. I don't know about you, but I enjoyed my burger and fries."

"I did too! Stop complaining!" another stated.

The woman grunted and moved along still grumbling under her breath.

Benedicto had gone ahead and found an area and provided it with cabins for the people in a large plot of land that was previously vacant. Each person would have their own cabin with everything they would need to live.

When they arrived at the lot, they saw the cute little cabins with colorful flowers outside each one in pots and a man and woman waiting for them. The couple were told of the arrangement and given control of the cabins and watching over these people who would be residents there. The couple had agreed to do this for the LORD and would be rewarded soon.

The couple came forward and greeted everyone warmly, "You can each take a cabin and get settled. These are our cabins and we are here to help you in any way you need assistance."

"What? Are you charging us for all this? I can't afford this!" the disgruntled woman announced with a frown.

"No, it is all taken care of. You can live here free and clear. Someone has already taken care of everything. You will have to work to help keep this place spic and span though. If you don't, you will lose your cabin."

"What do we have to do?" one man asked as he eyed a blue cabin down the end of the row.

"You will have jobs to do, each one of you. My husband will give them out to you once you are settled."

The people rushed forward to claim their cabins by pushing and shoving their way there.

Benedicto called out in a loud voice that reverberated all around, "Stop right here! You will not choose a cabin in this manner!"

All the people stopped and turned to look at the giant man who appeared to be growing in front of them with his booming voice.

"Um...okay. How do we choose our cabin then?" one man asked meekly.

"I will choose one for each of you. Come with me." Benedicto placed each person and family in cabins without too much distress on anyone's part. Once all were settled, he turned to Branyrd who stood with Ricardo holding tightly to her hand and looking lost and frightened.

"Where am I going to live? What about my parents? They won't know where I am when they come back," Ricardo asked frantically.

Branyrd bent down to speak with him. "I have something sad to tell you, Ricardo. Your parents were sick and went to Heaven. They are now with the LORD. HE is watching over them and you."

"I…I don't understand. What am I going to do?" Ricardo cried and dropped down to his knees.

Branyrd lifted him up and hugged him close as he wept for several minutes. She wiped his tears and gave him a tissue to blow his nose.

"I have good news also for you, Ricardo. Do you see that nice man and lady over there?"

"Yes, they are the ones who said everyone has a job to do. Does that mean I have a job too?"

"Well, possibly," Branyrd chuckled. "But they want to meet you. They don't have any children of their own and want to take care of you if you will let them."

"I guess so," Ricardo said as he sniffled and dried his eyes.

Branyrd took his hand and guided him over to the couple who were waiting to meet him. Benedicto had explained the situation to the couple about the orphan boy and how he needed someone to care for him. They had been thrilled to help out and would follow all the necessary channels to keep Ricardo as their son if only he would accept them.

Ricardo shook hands with the couple after introductions and hung his head down.

The woman asked him, "Do you like chocolate chip cookies, Ricardo?"

"Oh, yes, I love them!" Ricardo answered and whipped his head up as he met the woman's eyes.

"Well, come with me and we can make some together. Our house is over there. She pointed to a large gray split level with black shutters across the street from the cabins with many flowers all over the front porch hanging in baskets that swayed with the wind. It had a white picket fence and low shrubs that hugged the long front porch.

As they got closer, he could see rocking chairs on the porch and a table with cups and a pitcher of something to drink. He hurried forward to see what it was for he suddenly felt thirsty. There was also a dog sitting on the other end of the porch who jumped up when he spotted Ricardo. It came over to the boy and licked his hands and face as Ricardo bent down to pet it.

The woman announced, "That is Shecky. He is a labrador retriever. He loves you already. He will be your dog if you want him."

"He will? I never had a dog before." Ricardo's eyes were glistening with newfound tears as he looked at Branyrd coming up the stairs toward him.

"Well, what do you think, Ricardo? Do you think you will be happy here with your new parents?"

He looked at the couple and nodded. "Can I give you a hug before you go, Branyrd?"

"Of course. I was expecting one, Ricardo." The Angel giggled and hugged him back encircling him with her invisible wings.

Ricardo stepped back and said, "Are you an Angel, Branyrd? I thought I felt something tickle my neck like a feather."

Branyrd leaned closer to Ricardo and whispered in his ear, "Yes, we both are, but don't tell anyone. It will be our secret. Okay?"

"Yep, okay. It will be our very own secret!" He gave Branyrd another hug and shook Benedicto's hand before turning to pet his dog and hug his new parents.

Benedicto winked at Ricardo and waved goodbye as he and Branyrd moved away from the happy family. The three were hugging each other and playing with Shecky, oblivious of anyone else around.

As the Angels passed by the cabins, they noticed the people were already working to keep their new homes in order. The Angels waved at them as the people looked their way. They called out to the Angels and said, "Thank you for everything!"

Branyrd smiled and walked further away before she and Benedicto flew into the air.

"I think Ricardo will be happy with these people. They really are good and kind, don't you think, Benedicto?"

"Yes, they certainly are. No worries, Angel. Ricardo will be fine. He has a dog now and that in itself brought a smile to his lips. Didn't you notice?"

"Yes, I did. Dogs are Heaven sent, Benedicto. They provide the lonely with friendship, the unloved with love, the unhappy with joy, the sick with comfort and most of all they are loyal and supportive of their masters always."

Branyrd nodded but didn't let her Guardian Angel see the tears that threatened to fall because she missed Ricardo already.

CHAPTER TWENTY-EIGHT

"What do you think HE will give us next to do, Benedicto?"

"I'm sure we will know soon enough, Angel."

The LORD suddenly called out to the Angels, "You must stop the violence at this next place."

The Angels looked down and saw a large brick building with other similar buildings around it and an extensive square where many people were gathered holding signs, marching, chanting, and pushing and shoving security guards around.

"What is happening here, Benedicto?"

"It looks like a school or college. The signs are mixed about other nations and freeing the oppressed."

"Let's go down and investigate. They are getting rowdy and violence is sure to break out soon."

The Angels stayed on the outskirts and listened to the crowd yelling at the school officials and security. Police were pulling up all around the area and trying to corral the students' holding signs.

Branyrd flew up over the crowd and called out to them, "Listen to the officers. If you do not calm down, many of you will be injured."

The crowd looked up as one when they saw a golden lady up above them hovering in the sky without anything holding her up. They whispered to each other. "Do you see her? How is she up there? What is holding her there? How is she doing this? Who is she?"

Branyrd waved her hands over the crowd to calm them down as the police stopped moving to look up at her also. Word spread throughout the complex to the students and the police that there was a woman flying above them. Their focus was on the woman now and not on the picketing students.

The Angel flew away and landed outside the ring of police. She walked into the crowd and waved her hands over all as she passed by them. Some dropped their signs and wandered away in a stupor.

The police watched in surprise at this happening and noticed the woman standing alone in the circle with all the abandoned signs at her feet. They went closer to the woman with the golden hair and light that emanated from behind her.

The Chief of Police stepped forward and asked, "How did you do that and who are you?"

"I told them to go home. That is all. I am known as Branyrd, HIS messenger."

"Well, okay, but what I mean is, how did you fly above us? And who is HE?"

"None of this makes sense, Chief," one officer stated as he observed the students leaving the area.

"Do you believe in a greater power than on Earth?"

"Well, I guess I do. But you didn't answer my question, miss."

"HE is the LORD of Heaven and Earth; through HIM all things are possible."

"What does all this mean?" the Chief asked in confusion.

"Well, it means that your prayers and those of others have been heard and are being answered."

"I didn't pray…well, maybe a little," the Chief sighed and rubbed his wrinkled forehead. "If you are HIS messenger, does that mean that you are one of HIS Angels?"

"Yes, and so is Benedicto."

"Benedicto?"

The Guardian Angel appeared beside Branyrd to the shocked and dismayed officers who kept exchanging questioning glances with one another and shaking their heads in disbelief.

"Now I have to believe what you say. No ordinary people could do what you both have just displayed in front of our eyes," the Chief stated, still dazed.

"We are happy to help you, Chief. We can see how hard you and your men try to protect everyone from danger, even if it is from themselves. Your jobs are not easy ones. HE knows that. That is why HE sent us here to assist you."

"Well, it looks like you were successful in stopping these people from doing any more damage to the property or to themselves. But what are we going to do when they return?"

"You will calm them down and talk to them. Take them aside a few at a time. If they do not listen and stop being a danger to themselves and others, then you will have to arrest them. Don't stop praying to HIM. HE listens to all prayers and will send help again when needed."

"Will you be coming back?" the Chief asked with pleading eyes.

"We don't know that. HE makes all decisions and will tell us if we are needed here again. Stay alert here for a while in case the picketers return."

"Yes, we plan to do that and try to clear out all these signs and meet with the president of the university to come up with a plan."

"Take care and stay strong in the LORD." Branyrd said as she and Benedicto waved and flew away much to the astonishment of the officers who watched in awe once again and blessed themselves, bringing a smile to the Angels' faces.

"We can only pray that these students will come to their senses and stop picketing and causing trouble for the colleges and universities with HIS help."

"Don't worry, Angel, HE is keeping watch."

HE answered, "Yes, nothing gets by ME, Angels. Now you must travel far once again. There are others who want to harm those who are in office."

The Angels were guided to the next part of their multifaceted Mission of Hope.

CHAPTER TWENTY-NINE

The Angels flew over an area where hundreds of people were gathering. There were a few others gathered on a stage in front of these people. It appeared to be a rally of some kind.

The Angels listened to the murmurs of excitement throughout the crowd as it continued to grow in numbers. Flags and banners were being raised with names of different people on them, balloons were being held and all kinds of hats and caps were worn by the attendees.

The crowd hushed as one man stepped forward on the stage and took his place behind the microphone. He began to speak as the crowd cheered his every word. He waved to the crowd and stepped aside for another man to do the same and then a woman was last in line to speak.

The people cheered louder than ever for her and she smiled and waved her thanks to the crowd. She began to speak using her hands to make a point when there was the sound of gunshots that reverberated all around the stage. The two men who had previously spoken fell and other men in suits came forward to shield the woman but not before she was hit by a stray bullet that entered her shoulder.

The crowd screamed in alarm and ducked to avoid being shot, covering their families and friends at the same time. The Angels dipped down to investigate and prevent any more injuries.

People were still screaming and rushing here and there as the Angels descended onto the stage where they went over to the two men who had fallen. The people did not even notice the Angels there until they saw a bright light on the stage.

Some called out, "What is that light? Where is it coming from?"

Benedicto flew up to investigate where the gunfire was coming from and immediately apprehended two men who were hiding in the bushes. He brought them out and handed them over to the authorities who were waiting close by.

One man asked, "How did you see us?"

Benedicto didn't answer but nodded to the police who thanked him for his help and added, "You really shouldn't have done that, sir. You could have been shot."

"Yes, I know but HE would have prevented that from happening."

"Who?" one office asked, befuddled.

"HE is the one who sent us here to assist you. HE heard your prayers and answered them."

"What? Are you some crazy person? Do you want to be arrested along with these two? Maybe you are one of them."

"No, I am not one of them." Benedicto guffawed as he flew into the air causing the men to gawk, point and almost lose control of the two perpetrators.

Others looked up and began to call out and point to the man flying over their heads. Many began to pray and bless themselves.

"What is happening here?" a woman asked in tears.

"Who are these people?" another asked in wonder.

Another cried out, "Are those men dead? Is she okay?"

Branyrd lifted the injured men up and handed them over to attendants in an ambulance. She had helped the men regain consciousness so that they could be helped further by the EMTs. They would not die but would need to spend time recovering from their wounds. The woman was escorted by her guards to the ambulance and would also survive to see another rally.

The Angels waved their hands over the crowds and calmed them down so that no one would panic and be injured moving away from the area.

Many others were too stunned to move and stayed there to watch the ambulances move away and the stage to be emptied of people.

News vans quickly appeared spreading around to speak with the people to get more info. While other news people followed the ambulances with the hope of speaking with the men and woman who were injured.

Soon the world would know about this attempted murder of three people in the limelight. Questions were being asked of many who were there, officials and spectators both, without any resolution being attained.

HE told the Angels, "This is not over yet. There will be others who will be killed or injured in similar scenarios. The world is upset and evil is spreading. All it takes is one to spread this evil. But it also only takes one good deed to spread good around to swallow up the evil. Your jobs are to squelch this evil by encouraging good to spread."

"We will do our best, LORD. Where do YOU want us to go now?"

"Go to the churches and begin to spread the word about what is happening here and that you need their help in prayers."

"Yes, LORD. We will do that right away," Branyrd bowed and spread her wings in flight along with Benedicto.

They reached the first church and entered, staying at the front of the church. There was a baptism taking place. They waited for it to be over before going forward to see the priest.

As they walked down the aisle past the family of the baby who was just baptized, the priest looked up, crossed his heart and bowed his head. He didn't look up until the Angels spoke to him.

"Please open your eyes, Father John." Branyrd pleaded.

"Oh, my GOD and Savior!" the priest exclaimed as he finally raised his head and opened his eyes. "HE has sent you here."

"Yes, HE has, Father John." Branyrd answered with a smile.

"You are not in any trouble, Father John," Benedicto added to calm him down.

"I am doing my best here but many are not coming to church anymore."

"Yes, HE has noticed this."

"What does HE want me to do about that?"

"HE has asked us to come to all the churches, not just to yours, to help spread HIS word in prayers. Can you do that Father John? Spread HIS word in prayers?"

"I will do all I can for HIM. In fact, I will contact all the other churches in the area of all denominations to do their part."

"That is what HE would want. Thank you. Do all that you can, for evil is spreading wide and overpowering the good that is all over the world."

"I will begin a prayer service and call the other churches to do the same. We can gather together and pray as one," Father John announced.

"That is more powerful, praying as one. HE will be pleased with your efforts." Branyrd touched Fr. John's hands which made the priest jump from the shock that he received. Fr. John suddenly felt lighter and less burdened by all he had heard in confessions from the people who were suffering. He felt energized to begin this work for the LORD."

Fr. John rushed to the phone and contacted all the churches in the area and told them to spread the word about a prayer service that will include all the denominations. The priest spoke of receiving the LORD's word to do this.

The Angels flew to other cities and towns and did the same to help spread the word of GOD. As they flew around the world, they noticed crowds forming in front of churches and in squares. They flew closer so that they could hear what was going on.

What they heard were people praying in different languages as others who were trying to stop them were pushed back by many more who were praying.

As the Angels passed by these crowds, they lit up the sky with stars in the night or rainbows in the day causing the people to look up in amazement. Their prayers increased in sound and clarity reverberating all around the world.

There were those who still wanted to spread their evil but found it more difficult to do, causing them to grow quieter.

Across the world children were praying in their homes and in schools. Parents were encouraging their children to get along with their siblings and others. Teachers were not seeing as much mischief or problems from the usual students as before. If there were a few that got out of control, the others quickly reined them in.

Something was happening all over the Earth. The evil that had once spread was slowly being curtailed by those who sought a better world.

Leaders were meeting to discuss how to prevent war erupting on their lands while peoples who were once oppressed were experiencing a chance to make a better life in peace, prosperity and safety.

But unfortunately, there were those who did not like what they saw happening. They would do all they could to cause harm and dissension and would stop at nothing to do this to the innocent ones.

CHAPTER THIRTY

The Angels spread the LORD's word far and wide and circled the globe many times to ensure that it was working and evil was diminishing.

There was still one spot on the globe that was darker than the rest. They went down to investigate.

HE called out to them, "Be vigilant, Angels. There is danger ahead. I am here to assist you."

Branyrd turned to Benedicto, "What do you think HE means? Can we handle what is down there?"

"I don't see why not if HE has our backs. I have yours and you have mine, right, Angel?"

"As always, Benedicto, as always!"

What the Angels saw when they landed was not what they expected to see. There was a large man standing there waiting for them. He called out, "Well, it's about time you came."

"What did you say?" Branyrd asked, confused.

"I know who sent you! I will not bow down to anyone. I have a place here that is under my control. I will not give it up."

"Do you understand why we are here?"

"Yes, Branyrd. I know you. I have watched you grow up into a lovely First Class Angel."

Branyrd looked at Benedicto with wide-eyes and asked the person, "Who are you?"

"I am known as Henni. I was once an Angel myself but did not listen to HIM. HE did not like that and ostracized me here. There are others also here like me. Only one is not here, but you know where he is."

"Yes, I do know where he is. Well, it is time to return to HIM and ask HIS forgiveness, don't you think?"

The person shook his head and laughed. "It is not that easy to ask. HE will never want me back into HIS fold."

"You can't be too sure of that," Benedicto replied.

"How do you know, Guardian Angel on High?"

"I don't know what HE would do but I know that HE is a forgiving LORD."

"Maybe, maybe not. I did some bad things and must pay for my mistakes. That I know."

"The most important thing to know is that you are sorry for your evils."

"Yes, I…I like to think I am but then again… I've watched the world changed too quickly toward evil. I knew that HE would intercept it all eventually, as HE did. I have tried to change but it isn't easy to do."

"Of course, we understand it is difficult to change. But this is something you must do in order to enter Heaven," Branyrd stated as she looked the fallen Angel in the eye.

"Well…I don't know how to begin. What about the others here?"

"They will do whatever you do. We need more Angels to assist in this mission. It has been all encompassing and difficult to complete but we have managed to please HIM so far. HE will be even more pleased if you join us now."

Henni, the fallen Angel, looked up at Branyrd and Benedicto and nodded, "I will do my best. I have been watching what is happening around the world. It frightens me. Can you believe that?"

"Yes, I can and feel the same way, Henni. What you need to do now is call all the other Angels here and speak with them about what everyone must do," Benedicto instructed.

"I don't think they will be happy with this plan. They have been anxious lately because of the darkness that is spreading. But now I can see some light returning to the world. Whatever you two have done, the world is changing for the better. I do miss interacting with HIM and doing HIS bidding. Many of us were on missions like you two are doing now. We made some mistakes and we are now ostracized here."

Branyrd looked up and prayed for some guidance not only for herself but also for Henni and the other fallen Angels.

HE listened to the Angel's prayers, nodded and responded, directing HIS words to Henni. "I am waiting for you, Henni, and the others. Come forward and speak to ME."

Henni didn't dare meet HIS glowing eyes but did as he was requested by the LORD. Others soon joined Henni and were commanded to kneel in front of HIM.

Branyrd and Benedicto excused themselves from the area so that Henni could speak his peace without their watchful eyes. He was nervous enough without an extended audience.

The other Angels waited their turn as they each knelt in front of the LORD and answered HIS questions as they bowed their heads in prayer.

The LORD gave each of these Angels a mission to guide others who are lost to HIM. Once they have completed their missions to bring the more hardened criminals to change their ways, they would be allowed back to Heaven.

HE waved HIS hands over the fallen Angels and gave them back their wings, much smaller than the ones they used to have. Their wings would grow with each good deed they completed until they were full grown once again.

Branyrd listened to the LORD explain what these Angels would be doing. She and Benedicto soon after continued on their way to fly over another area that was troubled with drug dealers who were hanging around the schools.

The next part of their mission of hope, save the children, was going to be trying. It may be too late tragically for some of the children already.

The Angels only hoped that they were not too late to save the rest of the children.

CHAPTER THIRTY-ONE

Branyrd went into the school and sought out the principal to discuss the problems they were having with drug dealers. The man feared for the safety of all the children who were so easily swayed to try something new, especially if it looked and tasted like their favorite candies.

"Are the men here every day, Mr. Sergy?" Branyrd asked the principal after introducing herself, Benedicto, and explaining the reason they were there.

The principal looked at the Angels in awe and couldn't believe that they were there to help. He answered finally, "No, surprisingly they are not. But these men are definitely here every Monday and Wednesday."

"Why those two days?" Branyrd queried.

"I think that is when they receive their large shipments of drugs. I do tell them to leave or I will report them to the police. Somehow this doesn't frighten them."

"Who is that man over there watching us?"

"Oh, that is our custodian. He comes in daily to see me and report anything suspicious with the kids in the gym and other areas. He has confiscated many drugs from them and their lockers."

"I would like to meet this man, Mr. Sergy. He could be most helpful to us since he knows all the kids and which ones have taken drugs."

"Carl is a wonderful man who loves his job and the kids. They go to him to share their troubles instead of their parents. The kids know that Carl will not share what they tell him but he does warn them that if they take drugs, he will tell me and I will in turn report this to their parents."

The principal called his secretary to instruct her to have Carl come into his office.

Mr. Sergy looked up to see a surprised look on his janitor's face as he walked in. He quickly reassured him, "You are not in trouble, Carl. I wanted you to meet some visitors. This is Branyrd and Benedicto. They have been sent here because of our prayers to GOD. HE listened and now we will need you to assist them."

"Me? What can I do? They are the ones with all the powers. I am a lonely sinner whose prayers will not reach HIM."

"That is where you are wrong, Carl. HE has heard you and has listened. That is why we are here to assist you in saving the children."

Carl fell to his knees and cried when he heard this. "I don't understand. I am not worthy to even stand before you both."

"There is nothing for you to worry about, Carl. We need your eyes and ears on the children at all times. If you see or hear anything about drugs, call out to us. All you have to do is whisper our names and we will come."

"Is this for real, Branyrd? Can you fly? I don't see any wings. Don't Angels have wings?"

"Yes, to all your questions. You cannot see our wings here on Earth. They are only visible to human's eyes when you go to Heaven or when HE makes them visible to humans. But believe me, we do have wings."

"I don't know what to say. I am speechless for once in my life."

"Calm down, Carl. We need to discuss who is taking drugs right now. If you see anything being passed around in the gym, study hall, locker room or on the schoolyard, let us know asap," Mr. Sergy specified.

Carl nodded to the principal and directed his question to the Angels. "Shouldn't you two be going after the men out there so that they cannot give any of their poison to the innocent children?"

"Benedicto will be taking care of that problem. But there are others who are selling and distributing the drugs from these men. We need to stop them as soon as we find them."

"Okay, I can do that. I was just coming in to tell Mr. Sergy about some drugs I found inside the tank of the toilet in the boy's room. I noticed the chain was not moving and found a plastic bag resting on top of the chain preventing it from emptying and refilling the water in the tank."

"Did you bring it with you, Carl?" the principal asked as he shook his head in dismay.

"Yep, here it is. It could be heroin or something else. The problem with these bags is, we don't know what is really in them along with the drugs. They add poison to some as a filler."

Branyrd sighed at this and took the bag from Carl. "I think it is a synthetic mixed with several different kinds of pills that they crushed together."

"How do you know that, Branyrd?" the principal asked.

"HE has told me. We need to check all the lockers and the children's bags before they leave today, Mr. Sergy, to make sure there are no more of these bags around."

"I agree, sir. It looks like some of the older kids may be selling to make some money from their fellow students."

"I was afraid of that," Mr. Sergy stressed as he rubbed his hands over his neck and stretched to relieve the tension."

"Don't worry, Mr. Sergy. We will stop these kids from selling and then help those who have already taken the drugs and may be addicted. We only pray that this isn't so."

"I will call a meeting of all the teachers and students in the auditorium in a few minutes. I want both of you to come with me." The principal led the way to the speaker to make the announcement for the assembly.

The halls soon filled with teachers and their students as they walked to the auditorium to hear what this assembly was about. Teachers and children stared at the beautiful woman with the golden hair and light streaming around her and the huge man standing next to Carl. They whispered to one another about who they could be and waved to their favorite custodian.

Once everyone was seated and had quieted down, the principal stood up and began to speak.

"We have two special visitors here with us today who would like to share some words about what is taking place on school property. I think you all know what I am referring to. Please give a warm welcome to Branyrd and Benedicto. They are here to help us rid the school of the present issues that have plagued our town as well as other towns."

Branyrd stepped forward and held the microphone that the principal had just handed her. She shook her head and said, "I will not need that. I think everyone will be able to hear me. If you can't, please raise your hands."

The Angel's voice spread around the auditorium loud and clear as she began to urge the children, "Please do not take anything from a stranger. There are people out there that will cause you harm and possibly death if you take anything from them. A bag of drugs was found on the school grounds and confiscated. We will be checking everyone's bag and locker before you leave. All of this will be reported to your parents. If you have anything in either place that can be harmful to your fellow students, I suggest you take it out now and hand it over to us. This is for your own health and safety. Police will be called about this also."

There were murmurs from the students as they looked at each other and appeared anxious.

The murmurs increased in tone as Benedicto walked up to the mike stand and stood next to Branyrd. He whispered to her, "I have sent the dealers away from the yard. The police are on their way here to make sure they do not return."

Branyrd smiled and nodded to him as she looked out over the sea of faces. She met their eyes if they looked like they knew something. She waited for someone to come forward.

When no one responded to her request to turn in the drugs, she and Benedicto walked amongst the children and looked at them closely. The Angels could read their minds and scan over all the older students to hopefully find something that would be helpful.

One student finally raised his hand and stood up. "I know where there are some more of those bags. They aren't mine though. The men selling them gave them out to several of the middle school kids. I refused to take one. My older brother lost his life when he took some of these pills last year. He…was…the same age as I am now – eleven."

"I am so sorry to hear that." Branyrd waved her hands over the distraught boy. "That was a smart thing to do, young man. You unfortunately learned a valuable lesson from your older brother." Turning toward the rest of the students, she asked, "Will those students who took the bags please stand up?"

First one then a few other students stood up looking clearly frightened as to what their punishments would be.

The principal called the boys to the stage and questioned each one. "Do you have the bags in your shoulder bag or in your locker?"

Each boy said, "Yes, I have some in my bag and more in my locker. What are you going to do with us? Will we go to jail?"

"Not unless you continue to sell or distribute these drugs to other students. If you do, then you will be arrested," Benedicto stated in a loud and firm voice that startled each student.

The boys shook their heads and covered their faces with their hands, fearful of looking at those around them.

Teachers were instructed to go to their classrooms and stand outside the students' lockers in question while Branyrd and Benedicto searched for the drugs. They found several bags of powdered drugs and other bags with miscellaneous pills.

The police were alerted to confiscate the drugs. All students then returned to their homerooms as the Angels met with the police and Mr. Sergy. The students' names were not given out since they were too young to be interrogated without their parents' consent. This would be dealt with by the principal who will meet with the students' parents later that day.

The Angels left the school after much thanks was shared by the principal and the police. It was now in their hands to ensure that the children did not take any of the drugs again.

Benedicto scanned the sidewalk in front of the school and spied two men who he had sent away earlier. He headed toward them and appeared to grow as he got closer to them.

Once the men spotted the giant of a man who was strangely growing larger as he stood in front of them. Benedicto repeated what he had said to them previously, "You will leave here and not return. If I see you here again, I will personally take you directly to the police station and make sure you are locked up."

"Who are you? Who do you think you are to tell us what we can or cannot do? We don't answer to you."

"No, you do not. But you do answer to a greater power – the LORD!"

Before the men could reply, Benedicto waved his hands over the men, sending them flying off into the bushes two blocks away. The terrified men sat in the bushes and rubbed their sore arms, legs and looked over bruises that would be more evident in the morning.

"How did he do that?" one astonished man asked another.

"I have no idea but I am not sticking around to find out. I'm out of here. There has to be a better way to make a living."

"Yeh, there is, dummy. Stick with us. If you go back and tell the boss that you are not selling any more, he will kill you."

"Maybe I just won't tell him and leave the country. I will drop off the bags at his place and escape."

"Are you crazy? He has men all around keeping an eye on every one of us. He doesn't trust anyone. Do that if you dare. It was nice knowing you, man."

The man left with his bag of drugs and never looked back. He had to get someone to help him because he knew that he was as good as dead now.

CHAPTER THIRTY-TWO

The other men left the scene to stand outside another school unaware that the giant was already there pointing at them to leave.

"This is just great! He is here now! How did he know where we were going? He must have flown on a jet here," one angry man stated.

"I don't know but maybe the other guy, whatever his name is, was right to leave and give this up. We are all dead men when we don't sell the quota he gives us. There is no way we will get any of this distributed with those two people in our way. Are they magicians or something?"

"No, stupid! Didn't you hear the giant say that he was sent here by the LORD. That makes him an Angel, a very big one at that."

"You might be right about that. How could he throw us like he did and then be here before we arrived? He definitely has help from …."

"From what?" another man asked in confusion. "Who is helping him?"

"I can't believe you! He is an Angel, that's why he can do what he has done. No ordinary man could do that."

"You can't believe all that mumbo jumbo!"

"Well, it explains why he is here and how he can perform feats like that. Maybe the dummy was right to run the other way. If we stick together and explain what happened here, maybe he will let us go."

"Are you crazy? Of course, he's not going to let us go. He will have all of us murdered. He has plenty of men out there who would stop at nothing to get rid of us."

"All right. Let's get out of here. We can find others to buy our products. These kids are too young and they don't have any money."

"That is true but if we get them hooked, they will have to get money from their parents to buy more without the parents knowing what they are buying. These are rich kids who have everything. They are spoiled kids and get big allowances to do whatever they want."

"That's right. I see them throwing money around like it is not important since they have more than they will ever need."

"Look man, I don't want to do this anymore. Remember that young boy who overdosed last year? Well, I will never forget that. I had sold him a few pills but didn't know that he would take them right away. He fell at my feet that day. I can't forget the startled look on his face and the foaming at his mouth. I couldn't help him. It was too late!"

"We remember. We got out of there as quick as we could before the cops came to investigate. They couldn't touch us then and can't touch us now."

"Are you sure about that?" a voice asked them as they looked around for who had said that.

"Who said that?" one startled man exclaimed.

"I think it would be a good idea if you all left this town or any other and never come back. I will be watching for you. If you come back you will go to jail for a long, long time. I assure you," Benedicto explained

"All right, we are leaving," the men replied, as they hastily disbursed and never looked back.

"I guess you took care of them without my help, Benedicto." Branyrd giggled as she stood next to him. "You know I always have your back."

"Yes, I can see that, Angel. Thank you. I wouldn't know what to do without you!" Benedicto laughed out loud, giving her his quirky eyebrow.

Branyrd cried out in alarm, "We need to go back to the school. Mr. Sergy is in distress. One of the kids just overdosed in the hall. The school nurse is having some difficulty resuscitating the boy."

"Let's get over there, Angel. I hope we are not too late."

When they arrived at the school, Mr. Sergy called them in and brought them to the boy in question who was laid out on a bed in the nurse's office.

The boy's complexion was pasty white and his lips were blue. Branyrd rushed over to feel the boy's chest and start compressions as Benedicto spotted some white dust on the boy's lips. He reached inside the boy's throat to retrieve the pills that were still there. Luckily, he hadn't swallowed all of them at once.

The two Angels worked on the boy as they waved their hands over his body to rid it of the poison. The boy stirred after several minutes and the arrival of EMTs whisked him away in an ambulance. He would make a full recovery and hopefully remember not to take anything like that again.

The nurse and the principal gripped the Angels' hands in thanks for saving this boy who had been clinically dead. They didn't question how the Angels had done this and knew not to ask them. They were just thankful and said a prayer for HIS compassion to bring the boy back to life.

The boy's parents arrived right behind the ambulance and followed it to the hospital, distraught over what had happened to their son. They would have many questions for the school as to why their son took the drugs and how he was saved.

The Angels flew from school to school in the area and widened their search for any more dealers who were loitering around. Word had gotten out about this giant of a man who had injured three other men when they didn't listen to him after he told them to leave the area.

Drug lords were out in force to find this man and kill him to prevent him from putting them out of business.

There were several men walking the streets who were looking for the giant. He couldn't hide forever. They would not give up until they put him in his grave. Little did they know that was not possible.

CHAPTER THIRTY-THREE

Branyrd listened to the LORD explain about the men who were out to get Benedicto. HE said to watch out for them standing in doorways, alcoves and ready to jump out at them.

Benedicto turned his eyes to all the doorways as they walked along the sidewalks. His eyes glowed, dispelling the darkness and uncovering two men who ran away once they were spotted. They had taken one good look at the giant and couldn't raise their guns. Benedicto also had frozen their hands in mid-air in case they had tried to shoot.

The men ran into the park where others were gathered. Branyrd followed them and flew up above to listen into their conversations.

"What's wrong with you guys? You could have shot him and finished this." The boss slapped each man across the face to wake them out of a stupor.

"Sorry, boss, but we couldn't do that even if we wanted to. Our hands were frozen to our guns and we couldn't move even the trigger finger."

"Have you all lost your minds?"

"No, boss. It's true we couldn't move our hands. That guy did something to us. I don't know who he is or where he came from but he is no ordinary man."

"No kidding. You just realized that, you idiot!"

"I don't care how many it takes to kill him, just do it! If you are unsuccessful one more time you will be the next to die!"

The men mumbled in horror at the bosses' words. They couldn't afford to fail again. They gathered together to come up with a better plan to put the man away.

"This isn't over yet, Benedicto. The LORD said they are coming for you," Branyrd exclaimed.

"I can see them now. There must be two dozen men heading this way. Do you have my back, Angel?"

"As always, Guardian Angel. I am here for you."

The Angels flew up above the men causing them to look up in alarm. They tried to get away as the two Angels flew closer to the men's heads and knocked them over like bowling pins.

They got up quickly and tried to fight back with their fists and guns drawn. The men once again found that they could not raise their hands to protect themselves.

Benedicto pulled the guns out of their hands with a wave of his large hand. The Guardian Angel picked up the guns and twisted them into knots making them unusable ever again.

When the men saw this, they turned tail and ran away, pushing and shoving each other to escape the wrath of the giant.

Branyrd giggled as she watched the men falling and getting up again as they tried to move faster. "Well, it looks like they won't be back anytime soon."

"I would hope they wouldn't try to come back again. But I know you have my back if they do, Angel." Benedicto smirked at her and folded his arms across his massive chest as he kept an eye on the retreating escapees.

"Angels, you are needed at the park. There appears to be a confrontation between many men," the LORD commanded.

"Let's go see what is happening there, Benedicto. It could be real trouble."

"I'll go this way and you go around and get behind them."

The men looked up when they heard the sounds of wings like a flock of birds flying low. One man exclaimed, "It's not birds, boss. It's those two people who we saw at the schools. He is the giant of a man who threw us into the bushes. Look at all my scrapes and bruises."

"Never mind your boo boos. What are you, a man or a mouse?" the boss yelled at the complainer quieting him down sufficiently enough to prevent anyone else from complaining.

Benedicto whispered to Branyrd, "Drop down behind them. They haven't seen you yet."

185

Branyrd dropped down without a sound and cleared her throat causing the men to turn around to see who was there.

"What are you men up to?" Benedicto asked, as Branyrd and he closed in around the men.

"What concern is it of yours? Who are you anyway?" one brave man asked as he stood his ground.

"I was sent here to clean up this area. It's time for all of you to leave. Don't think you will be accepted elsewhere either. There are others out there that will also stop you."

Branyrd smiled at the men and said, "I think you better listen to Benedicto. He knows what he is talking about."

"Who are you, golden lady?" another man asked.

"I came with Benedicto to complete a multifaceted mission. You are part of my mission."

"Are you with another gang trying to infringe on our territory?" one man who was in charge stepped forward to ask.

"No, HE sent us here. You need to clean up your act or you will suffer the consequences."

"What? Are you saying you are going to take us out? I don't think you stand a chance against all of us, little lady."

"Did you forget me?" Benedicto stepped closer and grabbed the man in charge off the ground by his collar and let his feet dangle and kick out in protest.

"Let me down!" the man screamed. "Help me, you idiots!"

The other men around him backed away and shook their heads ignoring their boss's cry for help.

"Will you promise to take your men with you and never return?" Benedicto asked, giving the man his most frightening stare.

"Okay, I give up. Let me go!" the man cried out.

"All right. Get out of here now!" Benedicto yelled out loud enough for all the men to hear.

They scrambled away with the boss in the rear trying to get past them.

A scream could be heard as the Angels were turning to leave the area now clear of trouble.

"Did you hear that, Benedicto?"

"Yes, time to investigate. It sounds like it came from behind us. It appears that someone else may need our help."

There were two young women trying to fend off two men who were grabbing them and twisting their arms behind their backs. The men pushed the women down into the bushes.

Branyrd landed next to the two couples and pulled the men away from the women. She told the women, "Call the police and stay over there until they arrive. We will take care of these men."

The men looked at the golden lady and the giant man who stood over them. "Who are you?" one man asked in dismay.

"We are HIS messengers. You have threatened these two women with bodily harm. You will not leave this area until the police arrive. It will be up to them to take you to jail."

"But we were only trying to kiss our dates," one man explained.

187

"Dates?" Branyrd quizzed them. "They didn't look like dates to me. That is not how you treat a lady on a date."

"Maybe we should ask the ladies if this was a date," Branyrd responded as she went over to the women and asked them.

"Are you kidding me?" one woman cried out. "We don't even know who they are. They were trying to rape us. We were heading home after work and they came out of the bushes and attacked us."

"Hmm, I see," Benedicto said as he picked up the two men and held them closer so he could look them in the eyes.

The men shivered as they tried to kick their way out of the giant's hands. "We…we…weren't going to hurt them," the man explained as his voice shook.

"I think otherwise, gentlemen. You are anything but gentlemen. You will not come back here or bother these women or any other women you see. Do you understand?" Benedicto warned.

"Yes, sir. We won't be coming back this way. Do we still have to go with the police?"

"Of course you do. You did try to harm these women in a heinous way. You will be punished for your evil ways."

The police, shortly thereafter, pulled up and saw two men sitting on the ground with wary eyes. The men kept looking around them for someone or something. The Angels had flown away leaving the women to explain what happened.

The women tried to explain how a giant man and a golden lady came to their rescue. The police shook their heads and pulled the men to their feet. They escorted all four down to the precinct to explain this in more detail.

The women were relieved to look up and see the Angels waving back at them. They waved and threw kisses in thanks. The women knew that they had escaped from being not only raped but possibly murdered by the men and owed their lives to the giant man and the golden lady.

CHAPTER THIRTY-FOUR

The fallen Angels were flying around the globe to dispel evil and make up for all the wrongs that they had done in order to earn a place in Heaven again.

They soared and dipped to frighten those who were trying to harm others. They walked the streets when they saw gangs gathering to cause trouble. They patrolled outside shopping centers to keep out those who were looking suspicious.

Word soon was out that there were otherworldly forces in the skies who were attacking those who were dangerous to others. Those individuals went underground afraid to come out.

The LORD was keeping a close eye on these fallen Angels and smiled as they kept righting more wrongs to earn their places back with HIM.

Different rulers who were contemplating war soon changed their minds when they faced these fallen Angels who stood their ground and would not leave until all arms were dropped and peace was restored.

The world became quiet now that the bombing and terror was finally at an end. People came out of their houses and looked around. There were no gangs hanging around and no drive-by shootings. They all sighed in relief and looked up to say 'thank you' to whoever their saviors were.

Branyrd and Benedicto smiled in relief at all the extra help that these Angels had provided. They knew now that their mission was coming to a close.

As usual, Branyrd could feel a tightness in her chest as she tried to keep the tears from falling when she would be leaving all her new friends.

She looked up and whispered, "LORD, will you allow me to see all the people we helped while we were here? I need to see how they are doing and if they need anything else."

"Don't worry, Angel. I will have a window for you to view all concerned. I assure you that I will keep an eye on all of them. If there is anything they need, I will see to it MYSELF. They have learned how to be self-sufficient, thanks to you and Benedicto. You have done a commendable job and had a most successful mission."

"Oh, thank you so much, LORD. We did our best to please you. It fills my heart to know that you approve." Branyrd bowed down and blessed herself. When Branyrd looked up HE was no longer there.

She called out to Benedicto, "Did you hear what HE said? HE is pleased with the work we completed here. I know it is going to be time to leave soon. I didn't want to ask HIM when that would be but I know it will be soon enough. HE also promised to open a window so we can see how our mission subjects are doing."

"Yes, I did hear that. In fact, I think now is the time we must leave. I told you that HE would be pleased with your performance. You have outdone yourself once again, Angel."

"With your help, Guardian Angel Most High! Only with your help!"

"You could have done all of this without my help, Angel."

"No, I don't think so. What about the jail and the escapees? I couldn't have forced them back into the cells like you did so expertly."

"Don't doubt yourself, Branyrd. HE would have provided you with the strength to do that on your own."

"Well maybe, but I wouldn't be as scary as you," she giggled as she watched the scrunched-up expression on Benedicto's face.

"I can't believe the faces you can make, Benedicto! You are too funny for words."

"I do my best, Angel, to keep you happy. I like to see you smile. It lights up everything around you."

"Aw, thank you, Benedicto. I don't know what to say."

"Oh, I don't believe that for a second, Angel. You are never at a loss for words."

"Like you said, I also do my best to keep you happy," Branyrd giggled.

"All I know is that you had my back; that is why I was successful in everything I did," Benedicto said as he raised his quirky eyebrow at her.

"Okay, but you also had my back, right?" Branyrd looked around but her Guardian Angel had made his infamous disappearing act.

"Where are you? I can't believe you left me in the middle of our conversation!" Branyrd sighed with a smile and a twinkle in her eye. She knew he would come back the minute she needed him, maybe even before. All she had to do was whisper his name and he would be beside her.

***

As Branyrd's mind roamed over all the aspects of their mission, she heard her name being called. She looked around and saw the fallen Angels standing in front of her.

"Sorry to disturb you, Branyrd. You looked deep in thought. We wanted to let you know that we have completed our part of the mission and will be waiting for HIS approval about whether we will be going back to Heaven or not," one fallen Angel stated.

"I'm sure HE will let you know soon. HE listens to you sooner if you pray."

Before Branyrd could say anything else to reassure them, the fallen Angels were on their knees and saying prayers in unison. They had nearly completed several prayers when the skies opened up and HE appeared in front of them.

HE raised his hands over their heads and told them to rise. The fallen Angels quickly got to their feet but bowed their heads not meeting the eyes of the LORD for fear of not being worthy.

"You have done all that I asked of you. The world is a better place because of your good deeds. I have a place for all of you once again but you must always remember why you were ostracized to begin with. It could happen again and this time you will not be allowed to return. Do you understand what I am saying?"

One fallen Angel responded with head bowed, "Yes, LORD, we understand what you say and why we must do your bidding always."

"Good. Now rise and look at ME. I promise not to burn you. Follow ME to your new home."

Branyrd and Benedicto watched in awe as the fallen Angels disappeared along with the LORD in a cloud of smoke that traveled up into the skies and left a cloudless blue sky behind.

"I think they will behave now, don't you, Benedicto?"

"I certainly hope they do. If not…I don't want to think about where they will end up."

"Me too! That is not something I ever like to think about."

"We should travel around to make sure that all is secure and quiet. I think HE would want us to do that, Angel."

"I think so too. I don't want to leave just yet. I will do anything to stay a little longer. I do love Heaven and want to return but not before I know that all our charges are doing well."

"I can see that, Branyrd. I know how you are when it is time to leave."

"I'm sorry, Benedicto. I can't help how I feel. I have come to love these people and aways want to make sure they are safe."

"I understand, Branyrd. You have a big, tender and loving heart. All of these people were blessed to be in your care. They will never forget what you did for them."

"Really? I hope they don't forget me."

"Don't worry, Angel, they won't."

CHAPTER THIRTY-FIVE

The Angels flew over all the areas where she and Benedicto had visited and noticed the people moving around without any disturbances. They did not want the people to see them so they kept under the cover of a cloud.

They continued flying around the globe and noticed the wars had stopped but people were milling about in confusion. She waved her hands over them to settle their nerves and allow them to find their way home and to their families.

There were some who were injured and unable to move from where they had fallen. The Angels flew down to assist them and lead them back to their homes.

In order to complete their mission, as they had done in the past, the Angels spread their arms around and wiped away the remembrances of them flying from all the people that they had come into contact with but leaving only those memories of them being there to assist them.

When they were sure that they had covered everyone, they flew up into the sky and looked at the Earth from above the clouds waiting for the LORD to summon them home.

They shared their thoughts about each place they had visited and how they felt about each.

"I think my favorite was seeing the children happy and the people working to help each other."

"Yes, I think you are right about that, Branyrd. It was good to see the smiling faces of everyone once they believed in themselves and that they could work together in peace and prosperity."

"You said that perfectly, Benedicto. I couldn't have said it any better."

"Yes, I agree with both of you, Angels," HE spoke, causing Branyrd to jump up in alarm.

"I'm sorry to startle you, Angel. But I couldn't help listening to both of you reminisce."

"Well, I guess we were doing that. I feel fulfilled by all of this but sad at the same time."

"I can see that, Angel. You shouldn't be sad because you have accomplished more than I thought possible, not that I didn't expect you to do all this and more."

"I see. You believed in me, LORD?"

"Yes, I do believe in you. I always have, Branyrd, and always will. That is why you are now not only Angel First Class but also you have earned golden wings. You will always be at my side."

"I…I…can't believe this, LORD! I am eternally grateful. I am at a loss for words."

"Haha, I can't believe that, Angel. You are never at a loss for words," the LORD tittered.

"I agree with you, LORD," Benedicto guffawed in kind.

"Now prepare to leave Earth and return to Heaven with ME."

"But…but…LORD, you promised that I would be able to see all our charges in a window before we leave. We couldn't really see them too well as we flew over the areas."

"Of course, I always keep my promises, Branyrd. Come with ME."

CHAPTER THIRTY-SIX

The LORD opened one window at a time to focus on each part of the Angels' mission. HE first came to the mother and family – Myra, Sonya, Caleb and Tyler who were busily helping their neighbors with building and bringing water and food to the workers, along with the others.

Branyrd tried to keep the tears at bay but was unsuccessful as she watched little Tyler look up suddenly, smile and wave.

"Can he see us, LORD?"

"Yes, I allowed him to say goodbye one last time. Wave back at him and let him know that you are happy for him. Don't let him see your tears."

"I am doing my best, LORD," Branyrd replied with a sniffle as she threw kisses to Tyler.

Next the window changed and focused on the town where the people had been harassed by drive-by shooters and looters of the shops. Branyrd observed Hannah, first aid worker and the caretaker of the people, helping them find homes and ensuring that they were well fed and safe.

Branyrd waved at everyone but no one looked up. "I guess they can't see me, LORD."

"No, I didn't open a window for them like I did for Tyler. Send them your thoughts and they will respond."

Branyrd did this and noticed that the people began to look up and bless themselves.

"It did work, LORD. I sent them my love." The tears began again as she tried to control them.

They watched as the courthouse came into view next as the judge sentenced many more people to prison for their evil deeds. Branyrd had previously whispered in the judge's ear about not being lenient, for these men would go out and do the same thing again if given freedom.

Arianne, Liam and Noah were seen now as they sat at tables in the shelter eating their dinner. The boys looked up and smiled after Branyrd sent them a thought that she was always watching over them.

Arianne looked up at that moment too after her sons told her that the Angel was watching over them. Arianne smiled and threw a kiss to Branyrd in response.

The Angel grabbed it out of the air and held it close to her heart with a big sigh.

Siarra, the newspaper reporter, was busy at her desk wearing a wide smile as she typed up her latest good-news report.

Branyrd sent Siarra a thought about keeping up the good work and keep smiling.

Siarra smiled even more now and nodded her head as she looked up and patted her heart in thanks.

The window got larger to encompass all the hostages that the Angels had rescued. They were happy, healthy and back with their families. She sent them good wishes to stay well and safe.

Many women who had been trafficked and raped by their captors were now living in a safe house, getting rehabilitated from their drug dependencies and learning how to live in a safe environment.

Well wishes were sent their way as the women smiled and blessed themselves.

The homeless people that were given cabins were happily keeping them clean and assisting one another. The Angels watched as the orphan boy, Ricardo, who now had new parents, was playing in the yard with his dog, Sheltie. He had grown a couple of inches, had filled out and looked healthy and happy in his new home.

Branyrd whispered to him, "Enjoy your new home, Ricardo, and remember to always be kind to others and listen to your parents."

Ricardo looked up, puzzled at first, but then smiled and nodded before throwing another ball for Sheltie.

The window changed again and now showed a school where drug dealers had been staked out in the past. It was all clear and the children were happily playing in the yard. Several other schools filled the screen with the same scene playing out – happy children and safe streets.

The LORD opened the window to display the park where two women were nearly raped by gangs. The women were now back with their families and the park was full of families walking around with their dogs or sitting on benches eating. All looked peaceful and safe now.

Colleges and universities were now cleaned up of the abandoned signs and students were walking around returning to classes without any disruptions from picketers. Police could still be seen keeping a close eye on the areas.

The window focused on the area of the political rally where three prominent people were shot. These people were now healed and back to their jobs but warily keeping an eye out whenever they attended another rally.

The window displayed all the areas where people were now praying in and outside of churches. Everyone was gathering together from different denominations with their voices joined in unity.

Last but not least, the window revealed the fallen Angels as they flew around righting wrongs. The LORD smiled as HE watched the evil dissipate and the world become brighter without the darkness that once surrounded it.

"Well, it looks like your mission was a great success, Branyrd. It is time to return to Heaven. Are you ready?"

"Yes…I guess I am, LORD. But I will miss all my new friends here. Will I ever return again for more missions?"

"That I do not know, Angel. We will see how the world does now that you have touched it with your Missions of Mercy,

Love and Hope. People will eventually learn how to get along or not. You have done some wondrous things while on Earth. We hope that they will learn how to live in peace and love."

"Oh LORD, I think they will. But I will be ready if YOU need me to return and take on another mission though."

"I know you will, Angel. I know you will. But you will be at MY side to assist in helping those who come through Heaven's Gates. You will be there to greet them."

"I will? I didn't realize that was to be my new job. I can't believe it! You have made me a happy Angel beyond imagination."

"I'm glad to hear that, Branyrd. You will be kept busy as more and more come through the Gates. You may even meet some that you have already met during your missions."

"Oh, my! Yes, I remember there were some that YOU mentioned who were going to come soon. I hope they remember me as I remember them."

"No worries there, Angel. No one forgets you once they meet you!" The LORD'S titter reverberated all over Heaven as HE settled down at HIS throne.

EPILOGUE

Branyrd, Angel First Class, with golden wings, stood at the gates of Heaven with Peter who was in charge of looking over all who came to enter the gates. She was his assistant and greeter to welcome them home.

Many came uncertain as to what to expect. Once they were certified by Peter, the gatekeeper, Branyrd guided them to their final resting places to be with family who had passed before them.

She never tired of seeing the joy in their faces as they spotted their families and rushed into each other's arms. She couldn't cry now that she was in Heaven. There were no tears, sadness, heartache, evil or anything like on Earth to disrupt the peace and tranquility of this final resting place, only those who were good and had earned their way lived here.

Branyrd was so busy watching the families interact and chat away that she hadn't heard an elderly man call out to her in surprise. She turned to see who it was. She rushed to his side and guided him as he suddenly became young in front of her eyes. Everyone was young once they passed through the gates of Heaven.

"Do you remember me, Branyrd?" the man asked, presenting his broadest smile to her.

"Yes, I do, Brett. If I hadn't seen you older first, then I might not. How are you doing? You were part of my second mission. I remember that your sister, Sanora, took you in after finding you in the shelter you and the others built."

"Yes, she was good to me. I was blessed to have Sanora in my life even if it was only for a short time. I think she is probably taking my death quite hard. Will you check on her to make sure she is doing okay?"

"Yes, of course, I will. I will reassure her that you are being taken good care of by HIM. There is no better place to be."

"I can see that now. I was confused and frightened when I knew that I was dying. If I had known how beautiful it is here, I wouldn't have wasted time worrying about it. It is like nothing I have ever seen before."

"That is understandable. No one knows what Heaven is like until they come. But they also never return to Earth to tell others about how special it is."

"But I think I did see a little of it in a dream when my wife appeared. She told me that she would be here to welcome me home. I can't wait to see her. Is she here now?"

"Maybe you better look more closely over there." Branyrd pointed to a woman who was smiling at him with her arms opened wide.

"You are here! I knew you would be here waiting for me. You told me in my dream. I've missed you so much. It has been so long."

"Yes, dear. Now we will be together for eternity. Come with me. We have a home here. I can't wait to show you around. There is indescribable beauty everywhere that I could never describe to you in a dream. It wouldn't do justice to what you will see and feel once you were here."

Branyrd watched Brett, the marine who had been addicted, finally arrive to be with his loving wife. He was looking young and handsome and quite happy to be here. She sighed as she went back to the gate to welcome home more saved souls.

Two more familiar people entered the gates as Branyrd came forward to welcome them. They cried out with joy when they saw her. They were no longer old and affirm but standing tall, beautiful and handsome as Branyrd looked them over.

"You are here, Branyrd! We have missed you so much after you left us. Now we can see you every day. Do you remember us?"

"Of course, I know who you are. You are Mortan and Miriam from Candle Island. You are both so young and beautiful. It is good to see you both so strong. I've missed you too!"

The trio hugged and parted as Branyrd explained that there were others waiting to see them. She pointed at the family members who were waving at them. Once the couple spotted their parents, they bade goodbye to Branyrd and hurried to meet them.

There were many more coming through the gates as Branyrd turned back to assist them to their new homes. She smiled and sighed happily as she couldn't think of anything she would want to do more than to see all the people she loved while she was on Earth. She knew that many of them would not arrive for a long time yet, but in Heaven, there is no time factor, no clocks or worry about such things. Everything was done as it was supposed to be completed by HIM.

She would do all she could to make everyone comfortable and help them get acclimated to their new home in Heaven for where else would be as perfect as this. She would wait for the LORD to call her if or when she was needed once again to complete another mission on Earth.

"Good thinking, Angel!" Benedicto interjected through her thoughts.

"Thank you, Guardian Angel on High. I know you always have my back." Branyrd smiled and winked at Benedicto wherever he was.

"As you do for me, Angel!" he chuckled and went on his way but would always keep an eye on his favorite Angel.

THE END

ABOUT THE AUTHOR

Janice Spina is a retired administrative secretary from a public school system in Massachusetts. She has always loved writing poetry, novels, and children's stories. She published her first book in 2013 and has not stopped since.

This is the 47th book Janice has published. She also has two mystery series for middle-graders and preteens of six books each, one for boys and the other for girls even though they are enjoyed by both boys and girls. She has a fantasy series of three books with more to come for YA.

Janice has published 22 children's stories for young children. She also writes under J.E. Spina and has now published eight novels and a short story collection for 18+.

She can be reached at these links.

Website: http://Jemsbooks.com
Blog: https://Jemsbooks.blog
Twitter: http://twitter.com/janice_spina
FB Main Page: http://facebook.com/janice.spina.9
FB Author Page: http://facebook.com/janicespina7
FB Novelist Page: http://facebook.com/jespina7

Janice lives in New Hampshire with her husband, John, and two tanks of fish. John is the illustrator of her children's books and designer of all her book covers.

If you enjoyed this book, please leave a review where you purchased it and spread the word to your family and friends.

Janice loves to hear from readers and welcomes reviews from wherever her books are purchased. She says, 'It's like Christmas each time I receive a review!'

If you would like to be on Janice Spina's email list to receive updates, newsletters, and special deals on books, please follow her at her blog/website above.

Watch for more books coming from Jemsbooks.

A NOTE FROM THE AUTHOR

I hope that you enjoyed this story about an unforgettable Angel. This is the fourth book in this series. I infused some comedy into this fictional story. It deals with many issues that are evident in our world today. I hope you will find it entertaining and that it lightens your load, lessens your troubles, and allows you to laugh even in difficult circumstances.

There is so much unrest in our troubled world today. I don't have all the answers or solutions to fix the problems we have but I created this Angel to do this in her own inimitable way. I think Branyrd will give readers a little hope, love and inspiration to try to do their best and help others in need, let us know that we are not alone, and that HE is always watching over us.

This series is written for young adults – Ages 17+ but younger teens may find it entertaining too. I hope you enjoyed this work of fiction.

Thank you for purchasing one of Jemsbooks. I appreciate your kind support of me and my books. If you like this book, a review would be greatly appreciated wherever you purchased it. Reviews and word of mouth are the best way to spread your thoughts about books. Please share your review with friends and family. Reviews are valued and appreciated by authors.

I would love to hear from you. You can reach me at jjspina(at)comcast(dot)net.

All my books are available on Amazon and Barnes & Noble. Watch for more books coming for all ages. There is always something brewing at Jemsbooks.

With Blessings & Love,

Janice Spina

OTHER MG/PT/YA BOOKS BY JANICE SPINA for 10+

Davey & Derek Junior Detectives Book 1: The Case of the Missing Cell Phone
  Pinnacle Book Achievement Award,
  Honorable Mention- Readers' Favorite Book Award

Davey & Derek Junior Detectives Book 2: The Case of the Mysterious Black Cat
  Pinnacle Book Achievement Award

Davey & Derek Junior Detectives Book 3: The Case of the Magical Ivory Elephant
  Pinnacle Book Achievement Award
  Readers' Favorite Book Awards – Silver Medal

Davey & Derek Junior Detectives Book 4: The Case of the Brown Scraggly Dog
  Top Shelf Book Awards – First Place
  Finalist in Red City Review Awards
  5-Star Book Review – Readers' Favorite Book Awards

Davey & Derek Junior Detectives Book 5:
The Case of the Sad Mischievous Ghost
   Pinnacle Book Achievement Award &
Authorsdb
   Cover Contest – Silver Medal

Davey & Derek Junior Detectives Book 6: The
Case of the Mystery of the Bells
   Pinnacle Book Achievement Award
   Finalist – Readers' Favorite Book Awards
   Finalist – Book Excellence Awards

Abby & Holly School Dance
   Pinnacle Book Achievement Award
   Bronze Medal from Readers' Favorite Book
Awards

Abby & Holly Series Book 2: Unfortunate Events
   Pinnacle Book Achievement Award
   Readers' Favorite Book Awards – Honorable
Mention

Abby & Holly Series, Book 3, Secrets of the
Trunk
   Pinnacle Book Achievement Award

Readers' Favorite Book Award 5 Star Review

Abby & Holly Series, Book 4, The Hidden Stairway
Pinnacle Book Achievement Award
Readers' Favorite Book Award 5 Star Review

Abby & Holly Series, Book 5, The Copper Key
Pinnacle Book Achievement Award

Abby & Holly Series, Book 6, Faulty Timeline
Pinnacle Book Achievement Award

YA BOOKS BY JANICE SPINA for 15+

The Legend of the Taken Ones (Gateskin Chronicles Book 1)

…Mom's Choice Awards Winner - Gold Medal

5-Star Review from Readers' Favorite Book Awards

Finalist - Book Excellence Awards

The Unknown Territory (Gateskin Chronicles Book 2)

…Mom's Choice Awards Winner - Gold Medal

Search for the Medallion (Gateskin Chronicles Book 3)

…Mom's Choice Awards Winner - Gold Medal

BOOKS BY J.E. SPINA FOR 18+

Hunting Mariah

  (Finalist in Authorsdb First Lines Contest)

  (Maincrest Media Award) – Crime Fiction)

Mariah's Revenge

  (Finalist in Authorsdb First Lines Contest)

How Far is Heaven

An Angel Among Us: A Short Story Collection

In A Second

Lubelia Alycea: One Hundred Years

The Misunderstood Angel: Branyrd the Angel Series Book 1

Mission of Mercy: Branyrd the Angel Series Book 2

Mission of Love: Branyrd the Angel Series Book 3

www.ingramcontent.com/pod-product-compliance
Lightning Source LLC
Chambersburg PA
CBHW071157260626
47162CB00003B/1084